Dear Reader,

Home, family, community and love. These are the values we cherish most in our lives—the ideals that ground us, comfort us, move us. They certainly provide the perfect inspiration around which to build a romance collection that will touch the heart.

And so we are thrilled to offer you the Harlequin Heartwarming series. Each of these special stories is a wholesome, heartfelt romance imbued with the traditional values so important to you. They are books you can share proudly with friends and family. And the authors featured in this collection are some of the most talented storytellers writing today, including favorites such as Roz Denny Fox, Amy Knupp and Mary Anne Wilson. We've selected these stories especially for you based on their overriding qualities of emotion and tenderness, and they center around your favorite themes—children, weddings, second chances, the reunion of families, the quest to find a true home and, of course, sweet romance.

So curl up in your favorite chair, relax and prepare for a heartwarming reading experience!

Sincerely,

The Editors

K.N. CASPER

Ken Casper, aka K.N. Casper, is the author of more than twenty-five novels, short stories and articles. Born and raised in New York City, he's now a transplanted Texan. He and his wife, Mary, own a horse farm in San Angelo. Along with their two dogs, six cats and eight horses—at last count!—they board and breed horses, and Mary teaches English riding. She's also a therapeutic riding instructor for the handicapped. You can keep up with Ken and his books on his website, www.kencasper.com.

HARLEQUIN HEARTWARMING

K.N. Casper

Roots in Texas

HARLEQUIN® HEARTWARMING™

Recycling programs
for this product may
not exist in your area.

ISBN-13: 978-0-373-36625-5

ROOTS IN TEXAS

Copyright © 2013 by Kenneth Casper

Originally published as AS BIG AS TEXAS
Copyright © 2005 by Kenneth Casper

This edition published by arrangement with Harlequin Books S.A.

For questions and comments about the quality of this book,
please contact us at CustomerService@Harlequin.com.

® and TM are trademarks of Harlequin Enterprises Limited or its
corporate affiliates. Trademarks indicated with ® are registered in the
United States Patent and Trademark Office, the Canadian Trade Marks
Office and in other countries.

Printed in U.S.A.

HARLEQUIN®

www.Harlequin.com

Roots in Texas

This story is dedicated to all the members of PATH International, the Professional Association of Therapeutic Horsemanship, and their hundreds of volunteers who contribute countless hours to help children and adults meet the special challenges in their lives. Of special note is their Equine Services for Heroes program for our wounded servicemen and women.

CHAPTER ONE

"MEGAN, DO YOU HAVE your inhaler?"

"Yes, Mommy." The eight-year-old patted her black patent-leather purse, her latest acquisition.

"If you have any trouble breathing, I want you to use it right away and tell me," Kayla instructed her. Megan would use it if she had to, but she wouldn't make a public display of it if she could avoid it.

"You know horses don't bother me, Mommy," Megan insisted. "I've been riding for a whole year now, ever since Daddy let me sit on that pony for my picture, and I haven't had to use my inhaler even once."

"That was in Oregon, honey. We don't know if you'll react that same way here in Texas. We have to be very careful."

The fact that her ex-husband let their daughter sit on a horse, when he'd been told cats and horses were the worst triggers for asthmatics, still riled her. Daryl seemed to think ignoring

Megan's illness, or pretending it didn't exist, would make it go away. The kitten he'd brought home should've taught him otherwise. Megan's reaction had been so severe she'd ended up in the emergency room on a forced-air machine. He—or rather Megan—had been lucky in the case of horses that she hadn't had an adverse reaction. In fact, for the past year she'd been riding almost every week and doing fine. The first sign of troubled breathing today, though, they'd be out of there for good.

"Mommy, what color is Birdsong?"

"I don't know, honey. Mr. Tanner didn't say."

"I hope she's gray. I really like gray horses. Is she very big? I like big horses, too."

"Mr. Tanner didn't call Birdsong a pony, so I imagine she's a regular-size horse." Kayla just hoped the mare would be suitable and available.

She slowed as she approached a break in the wire fence that stretched on as far as the eye could see, up and down the low, rolling hills. A rustic wooden sign announced The Broken Spoke. She turned left. The car rippled over a cattle crossing.

The rooster tail of dust her aging Toyota was kicking up on the dirt road reinforced just how completely different this Texan countryside was from the damp and rainy coast they'd left behind. Kayla missed the tall trees and snow-covered mountains she'd grown up with, but the doctors had insisted Megan needed a drier climate. The girl had been considerably better since they'd moved here a month ago, and Kayla had to admit there was an unexpected beauty and charm in this wide-open land, a sense of boundless freedom that was invigorating, and she was delighted by the friendliness of the people. Megan, of course, was thrilled to see real live cowboys.

Over a low rise Kayla spied a ranch house in the shade of what she'd learned were live oak trees. Behind it was a big wooden barn and a cluster of smaller metal buildings. She rolled to a stop in the gravel parking area beside the barn, her eyes instantly drawn to the man in the middle of the corral opposite. He was quietly approaching a horse. The horse was staring white-eyed back at him.

Unbuckling her seat belt, Megan jumped out of the car, slammed the door and took off for the enclosure.

Startled, the horse tossed its head, neighed and sidestepped skittishly away from the man.

Kayla saw him slouch in frustration. Uh-oh, not a good start.

"Megan, stop right there!" she called out.

The girl hesitated, then reluctantly obeyed. When Kayla caught up with her, she took her hand and together they cautiously approached the pipe fence.

"Is that Birdsong?" Megan asked.

"I don't know, sweetheart, but you can't go racing around here, disturbing things."

The man in the ring was tall, slender and wore work-faded jeans with a large silver belt buckle, plaid shirt and cowboy boots. All that was missing was the Stetson.

He sauntered over to them.

"What can I do for you?" He wasn't unfriendly, but somehow his tone lacked the warmth she'd come to associate with Texans.

"I'm sorry we spooked your horse."

He glanced over his shoulder at the mare in the far corner watching him suspiciously.

"No permanent damage done." His voice was a mellow baritone with just enough Texas in it to be charming.

"Is that Birdsong?" Megan bubbled.

"Birdsong?" He gazed at her, and it seemed to Kayla there was sadness in his eyes.

"I'm going to have my very own horse. Mommy promised."

Time to take control of the situation. Kayla

extended her hand. "I'm Kayla Price. This is my daughter, Megan."

She wasn't surprised that his hand was rough and callused. He was, after all, a cowboy. It was also large and warm, the grip firm but surprisingly gentle.

"Ethan Ritter," he said. "Y'all must be the folks who've taken over the Conyer place." He started walking toward the gate. Kayla followed suit on her side of the fence, Megan skipping along a pace or two ahead.

"Actually, just the house and forty acres."

Lifting his hat from a fence post, he pushed it down over his thick brown hair, opened the gate and secured it behind him. "What are you planning to do with the land?"

"Grow grapes. We're calling it Stony Hill Vineyard."

He didn't look shocked and he didn't laugh, which she took as a good sign. "Why a vineyard?"

"Why?" she repeated. "Why not?"

"Not a good answer." He kept walking toward the weathered barn.

Kayla found herself practically jogging to keep up with his long stride. His dismissive attitude had her pulse up. "Excuse me?"

"You need to have a positive reason for

doing something if you want to succeed," he explained. "You won't accomplish much with that negative mind-set."

"Are you always so judgmental?"

"Gee, I hope so," he said with an aw-shucks grin. "Isn't that why the Good Lord gave us intelligence? To make decisions, judgments?"

She didn't know what to say. Most people took the word *judgmental* as a criticism; he was wearing it like a badge.

"Are we going to see Birdsong now?" Megan asked, bouncing up and down.

Ethan slowed and smiled at her. "Sure, you can meet Birdsong. We'll have to call her in from the pasture, though. She's busy right now snacking on green grass. Would you care for a drink of water?" He worked his mouth, clucking his tongue. "I'm dry as a bone."

"Yeah, me, too," Megan said, very adult. "Dry as a bone."

He grinned with unexpected affection, and in spite of her pique, Kayla couldn't help smiling, too. She liked the way his expression softened when he spoke to her daughter. He was definitely opinionated, but there was a childlike quality about him, as well. An intriguing combination, she decided, and a dangerous one.

The barn's rich scent of hay and feed nearly

overwhelmed Kayla as Ethan led them into a small room, its rough wooden walls covered with racks of saddles and tack. Over by a battered school desk he took three bottles of water out of a small refrigerator. Twisting the cap off one, he handed it to Megan, gave the second to Kayla and then downed half of his in one long draw.

Kayla tried not to stare at his Adam's apple as it bobbed with each swallow.

Back outside, he showed them to a large pasture where half a dozen horses were grazing. Two fingers between his teeth, Ethan whistled, and the animals began to saunter toward him.

"The bay in the lead is Birdsong," he explained.

The brown horse had a black mane and tail, as well as four black stockings. She also appeared to be bigger than the others.

"She's beautiful," Megan declared. "I don't care if she's not gray."

Ethan looked at Kayla.

"That's her favorite color this month."

Again, he smiled. Oh, yes, definitely dangerous. A woman could grow very fond of that smile.

Megan moved down the fence to where the animals were headed.

"She's horse crazy," Kayla explained.

"A lot of kids go through the phase at that age. How old is she, about eight?"

Kayla was impressed. Most bachelors were poor judges of a child's age.

"Yes," she responded. "She has pictures of horses all over her room, statues on her shelves and has nagged me into subscribing to every horse magazine she can find."

"Give her a few years. Once adolescence hits and she discovers boys, horses will quickly be forgotten."

"The opposite sex doesn't seem to have distracted you," she blurted, blushing when she realized what she was saying.

He tilted his head in amusement. "I'm not immune." His green eyes studied her, making her decidedly uncomfortable, a condition he obviously enjoyed, because he laughed before observing, "I have more than a dozen horses here. What's your interest in this particular one?"

"When I was in the general store yesterday, I happened to mention I might be interested in buying Megan a horse. Mr. Tanner said your Birdsong was very gentle with kids, and that you probably didn't have much use for her anymore."

For a moment Ethan's expression shifted,

but the sadness, if that's what it was, vanished when the big mare came up to the fence and nosed his arm.

"Can I pet her?" Megan cried. "Can I? Please?"

Ethan beckoned to her. "Come here."

Wide-eyed, she rushed over. He lifted her so her feet rested on the bottom rail of the fence. "Put your hand out slowly with your palm up and fingers flat, and let her sniff you for a few seconds. Then you can rub her nose."

Megan did what she was told, then giggled as she ran her fingers above the horse's nostrils. "She's so soft," she said in amazement.

"That's the silkiest part of any horse," Ethan told her. "Now slowly move your hand up to her forehead. You can feel her coat there is rough."

Kayla held her breath and watched for any change in Megan's breathing. None.

"If you really want to make her feel good, rub her just above the eyes. Like this." He cupped his hand over the horse's right eye and rubbed it in a gentle massage, then guided Megan's much smaller hand to do the same thing. "That's it. Nice and easy. Not all horses like to be touched there, but a lot of them do. I think Birdsong really likes you."

He had a way with children, Kayla decided,

and wondered why he wasn't married and raising a family.

"Can I ride her?" Megan pleaded.

"Maybe another time. She's ready to come
in for her supper now."

Megan's disappointment was palpable, but
to Kayla's immense relief she didn't push the
issue.

"Ready to bring them in?" asked a man behind them.

Kayla spun around. An older cowboy with a
paunchy middle and a scuffed straw Western
hat shielding his leathery face had approached
so quietly, she hadn't even heard him.

"Carter, this is Kayla Price," Ethan said
over his shoulder, still holding Megan so she
could run her hand over the horse's other eye-
lid. "They're interested in buying Birdsong."

Carter grunted and moved to the gate a few
yards down, where he removed one of a dozen
halters hanging on the fence. Birdsong instantly
trotted to him, nudging another horse out of
the way. No question about the pecking order.

"Can I go with her?" the girl begged.

Ethan let out a chuckle. "Carter," he called
over, "Megan would like to help you bring
Birdsong in."

"Don't need no help," the old man grumbled. "Been doin' this longer than you been alive."

Ethan just looked at the man with raised eyebrows.

"Oh, all right. Come on then. Don't have all day." Carter stepped inside the gate and put the halter on the big mare, who seemed to accept it eagerly. "Give her room," he barked at the girl, "if you don't want to get run down."

She jumped to the side as he brought the horse through the gate, crowding out the others in the process and latching it behind him. Kayla suffered a moment of anxiety looking at her daughter, so small beside the huge animal.

Kayla watched, smiling as they moved toward the barn. Megan was marching like a soldier, head up, utterly delighted in her role as official helper. Carter said something to her, and Kayla hoped it wasn't a reprimand. Then, to her surprise, he handed her daughter the lead rope. When Megan looked back, her face radiated pure joy.

Kayla couldn't help grinning. "He's made her day."

Amusement played across Ethan's lips, too. "Buy her a horse and she'll get to do that a lot."

"You think she'll tire of it then? You might

be right. Have you ever gotten tired of being around horses?"

For a moment he got that dreamy look in his eyes again. "No. Don't think I ever will, either."

He haltered the next mare.

"How experienced a rider is Megan?" The nostalgia was gone from his voice.

"Not very," Kayla admitted. "Back home I took her to weekly group lessons at a stable not far from where we lived. They taught English, but it was more for amusement than serious training. She's never been on a Western saddle, which is what she really wants—to be a real cowgirl."

"So she's a relative beginner."

"Afraid so. She'll be an eager student, though, I can promise you that."

"What do you know about keeping horses?"

"Not much." She walked on his left as they followed the same path Carter and Megan had taken. "We've never owned a horse, but I figure we can learn."

"Or kill the animal out of ignorance." His tone was sharp now. "What are the symptoms of colic?"

"Oh, I—"

"How about founder? Thrush?"

She listened to the clop-clop of the horse's

hooves on the gravel but said nothing. She didn't know the answers.

"How often does a horse have to be shod?"

She shook her head. "I don't know."

"You reckon you can just pick that information up from a book or magazine?"

"People do buy horses," she pointed out.

He shook his head in disgust. "How much do you plan to spend on this hobby?"

She chose not to respond to the implied put-down. "I don't know what you're asking for Birdsong," she said, "or if I can afford her. We have to start somewhere, don't we?"

"I meant, how much have you budgeted each month?"

She looked up at him. "I don't understand."

"I know you don't." They'd reached the barn. He stopped and studied her. "Mrs. Price, buying a horse is only the down payment on a variety of expenses. There are, for example, the vet fees. You can budget for shots, but not for the unexpected bills that come with unpredictable ailments. Colic is the most common. If it's in the middle of the night or on a Sunday or holiday, you shell out extra dough to call the vet out. By the way, do you own a horse trailer and truck strong enough to tow it? That car you drove up in sure won't handle the load."

Her dad had a truck, but it was a small one. She was spared answering as Carter and Megan passed them going the other way.

"I'm helping bring in the other horses, Mommy," Megan called out, clearly enthralled.

"That's nice, honey."

"You'll have farrier fees for shoes every six weeks or so," Ethan went on.

He led the horse into the barn. Inside a box stall he removed the halter. The mare immediately made for a bucket hanging on the wall and started chomping grain.

"Have you considered feed?" Ethan asked, closing and latching the heavy door and hanging the halter on a peg beside it. "What kind of hay? Coastal or alfalfa? How much oats? What kind of supplements?" His eyes surveyed the room.

"Then there's time," he continued. "Are you up to feeding twice a day seven days a week, rain or shine, wind or snow? You'll need to put the horse out to pasture every morning and bring her in every evening when the weather is fair. Do you have someone competent who can fill in for you when you're not available?"

They stepped outside. The early-February sun was going down and so was the temperature. Not cold but decidedly chilly.

"These animals are dependent on you for their survival," he emphasized.

"Other people do it," she insisted, but she began to wonder if she'd made a big mistake promising her daughter a horse of her own.

ETHAN HAD BEEN studying his visitor's reaction to his questions, or rather his relentless grilling. She wasn't pleased with him, but he suspected she was even more displeased with herself. She'd apparently promised her daughter something she now realized she couldn't deliver. A dilemma for any parent.

What about Megan's father? She hadn't mentioned him. Ethan had noticed she wasn't wearing a ring. He'd met a few married women who didn't, but Kayla Price didn't strike him as that type. Strong, independent, yes, but also one who took a commitment seriously and wasn't bashful about acknowledging it.

There he was being judgmental again.

Was she divorced, widowed, a single mother who had never been married? Not that it was any of his business. Her private life was her own.

One thing was for sure, he wasn't about to sell her Birdsong under any conditions. The mare was still sound—sweet, patient and gentle—

and would make an ideal horse for a little girl like Megan, but that could change quickly. If all went well, Bird might have another five years left. On the other hand, the next bout of colic could be her last. Ethan couldn't in good conscience sell a horse of that age to an incompetent buyer, even if he were inclined to part with her—which he wasn't.

"Look—" he tried to sound friendly rather than negative "—you're not ready to buy a horse. Maybe when you've had some experience and know what you're getting yourself into. Until then, I recommend giving your daughter lessons and leaving it at that for a while."

Kayla nodded, but she wasn't pleased. "I wish you weren't right," she admitted. "Megan is going to be so disappointed."

"And you'll be in the doghouse."

She caught his eye and smiled ruefully. "Big-time."

The girl approached leading a brown horse with three white stockings. "This is Izzy, Mommy. That's short for Isabel."

"She's going to have a baby in a few months," Ethan told her. "Maybe you can come back then and see the foal."

"Can I, Mom?"

"We'll see, honey."

"I've never seen a baby horse, except in pictures. Are they really cute?"

"As a button," Ethan assured her.

"The second stall on the right," Carter said and gave Ethan a disgruntled look.

Man, child and horse disappeared into the shadows of the old structure.

"Maybe we can settle on a compromise," Ethan told Kayla.

"What do you mean?"

"Tell Megan Birdsong isn't for sale, but I'd like her to ride the horse to see how well they get along. If she's still interested after a few sessions, I'll give you a half lease on her."

"Half lease? On a horse?"

He nodded. "You pay half the upkeep, including feed, shots and shoeing. Megan can ride her anytime she wants, whether she's taking lessons from me or not. I pay the other half, as well as anything unexpected that might pop up, like vet bills when she colicks. Your monthly tab will fluctuate according to the cost of feed and routine vet charges, but you won't have any catastrophic bills, and you can terminate the lease anytime you want."

"Sounds like a good deal."

"It is."

"Except Birdsong stays here, right?"

He nodded.

"That's the part she won't be happy about. She's been counting on having her horse in our stable."

"One other thing. You—or she—also do half the chores. That means coming over here every other afternoon after school and mucking out the stall. Might as well find out if she's serious about this horse business."

Kayla laughed. He liked the sound and the way her face lit up.

"Try it for, say, three or four months. After you've gotten a taste of the care and feeding of horses and have a better idea of what you're letting yourselves in for, if you still want to buy her a horse, I'll help you find one."

"But you said we were going to buy Birdsong." Hands fisted, Megan stomped her foot. "You promised."

"Megan, I said I would consider it if we could afford to and if Birdsong was available, but Mr. Ritter doesn't want to sell her. I can't make him."

"You promised," she shouted, red-faced. "You said I could have my very own horse. I love Birdsong and she loves me."

Under different circumstances Kayla might have laughed at her daughter's notion of instant love.

"Calm down, honey. You're going to make yourself sick."

Megan glared at her, her mouth pinched. She didn't often throw temper tantrums, but when she did they had serious consequences. Her breathing was already becoming rapid, raspy.

Kayla led her to a bench beside the old barn, sat her down and reached into her pocket for the extra inhaler she always carried.

"Here, use this," she said.

"I don't want it," her daughter all but shouted, though her voice didn't carry very well. "I want Birdsong." Her breaths were coming in quick inhalations now. But it was exhaling that was most difficult.

Ethan finished filling a water trough over by the corral and strolled over. Kayla had been aware of him watching them. "What's wrong?"

"Her asthma is acting up. She'll be all right in a few minutes." She again offered the inhaler.

Desperate now for air, Megan didn't refuse it a second time. She sucked in two draws from the small canister, and her breathing immediately began to ease.

Kayla stayed with her for a few minutes before getting up. "Wait here while I get your purse. I think you left it hanging near the gate."

Megan nodded.

Ethan trailed along beside Kayla. "Your daughter has asthma and you brought her to a stable. Don't you know horses can set off an attack?"

She looked at him, impressed with his knowledge of the disease, displeased by his holier-than-thou tone.

"She's not having a reaction to the horses, Mr. Ritter. She's brought this attack on by getting upset."

"What would have happened if she'd reacted to the horses?"

Kayla stopped and glared at him. "I would have taken her home immediately, put her on her nebulizer and not brought her back. As it is, I may not anyway."

"I can't believe you'd take that chance."

Kayla prayed for patience. "Mr. Ritter, I've lived with my daughter's health problems all her life. I'm well versed on what she can tolerate and what she can't. She's been around horses nearly every week for the past year without difficulty. Today has been no exception.

She's upset because she can't take Birdsong home. It'll pass."

He didn't look convinced.

"You offered to give her riding lessons a few minutes ago. Are you going to renege?"

"I didn't say that."

"Then you do your part, Mr. Ritter, and I'll do mine. Can we agree on that?"

He clearly didn't like being cornered. Daryl hadn't liked it, either, when she called him on commitments he'd made.

"Bring her Monday after school. If she has another attack, though, the deal's off."

ETHAN FINISHED hanging up the last piece of tack and scanned the room for anything out of place. Order had always been a trademark of the Ritter barns and stables under Carter Dunlap. The old man had been a ranch hand on the Broken Spoke long before Ethan was born.

Satisfied, Ethan turned off the light as he exited, only to bump into the old cowboy outside the door.

"What do you think you're doing?" Carter asked.

"Just finishing up."

"I mean about the girl."

"Giving her lessons. What are you so upset

about? We can use a few more paying customers."

"You can't change the past. I'd have thought you'd understand that by now."

"I don't know what you're talking about." Ethan started to walk around him, but the old man grabbed him by the arm with strength that was surprising and a bit frightening.

"It's over. She's at peace. Let her go. Torturing yourself won't do no good. Get on with your life."

Ethan yanked his arm away.

"It wasn't your fault," Carter called after him.

But it was his fault. Nothing could change that, either.

Ethan's heart was pounding as he strode toward the back of the ranch house.

Was Carter correct? Should Ethan put distance between himself and this girl with the uncanny resemblance to Angela? Was he trying to relive history…and get it right his time?

It didn't matter. He'd made a deal and he would live up to it.

CHAPTER TWO

"THE VINES SHOULD BE arriving around ten," Kayla's father reminded her over the breakfast table Monday morning.

"Looking forward to getting your hands dirty?"

He grinned. "Yeah."

Boyd Crawford had been skeptical when she'd found this land opportunity in Texas, but he'd supported her and agreed to come along for a few months to help her establish her first vineyard. He understood how desperately she needed to make a new beginning after Daryl had walked out on her and Megan.

Over the past month they'd identified the ten acres that had the best potential, the optimum incline and drainage. They'd tested the water, analyzed the soil and installed an irrigation system. Last week he'd flown to California and personally arranged for the shipment of select vinifera vines.

Texas boasted a growing number of flourishing vineyards. All Kayla's studies indicated this one should be equally successful.

"Finish your milk, honey, and then get your backpack," Kayla told her daughter. "The school bus will be here in a few minutes."

"I'm going to ride Birdsong this afternoon, Grandpa," the girl sang. She'd been grounded over the weekend for her temper tantrum at the Broken Spoke on Friday, yet that was all but forgotten.

"You be careful, now." He smiled at his granddaughter.

At this point Kayla wasn't sure she was as thrilled with the idea of Megan riding. Facing Ethan Ritter again wasn't something she particularly relished. The man had a sharp tongue, which was aggravating, and other aspects she found disturbing in a different way. His good looks, for instance. The shape of his mouth and the warmth in his green eyes made her entertain possibilities she thought she'd dismissed from her life when she'd divorced Daryl last year. Distractions she didn't have time for now.

She couldn't deny that she found Ethan's personality intriguing, too. He projected strength and self-confidence, but also vulnerability. He was obviously good with kids—at least he'd been with Megan—which added to his appeal.

Still, something about the man unsettled her, something she couldn't put her finger on.

He was opinionated and critical, yet she felt safe with him, perhaps because of the protective way he'd reacted to Megan. Whatever it was, it had her spending too much time thinking about the guy.

"We'll go over to the Broken Spoke right after you get home from school and change clothes," she told Megan.

She was tempted to add that this first lesson might not last very long but decided not to dampen the girl's enthusiasm. Megan would be preoccupied enough in class today without worrying about how long she'd get to ride her precious horse. "Now hurry. You don't want to miss the bus."

Ten minutes later the house was quiet.

"Are you sure about this riding business?" her father asked over his second cup of coffee.

"Maybe this is just a phase, like Ethan says, but, Dad, how can I deny her the opportunity to find out?"

"Is that what Ritter thinks?"

She didn't miss his use of the neighbor's last name. "He says adolescence will probably distract her—"

"Woo her away, huh?" He smiled at her over the rim of his cup.

"Something like that."

"How much time is this latest obsession of hers going to eat up?"

His tone was more amused than critical. Megan wanted to see and try everything. Most of the time her interest waned after the initial experience, but her fascination with horses hadn't so far, and his concern had merit. Work on the vineyard, this first year especially, would absorb all Kayla's spare time, another reason why Ethan had been right in discouraging her from buying a horse—for a while at least.

"Three one-hour lessons a week, Monday, Wednesday and Friday. We're only a few minutes away—it'll actually be less intrusive than having to take her to soccer or basketball."

Boyd drank down the last of his coffee and got up from the table. "I'm going to walk the lines one more time."

There was nothing wrong with the miles of wire they'd strung for the vines. But starting from scratch was a new adventure for both of them, and he was as nervous about it as she was.

"Thanks, Dad."

He turned at the door. "For what?"

"Being here for us."

His expression, often so intense and pensive, softened. "I'm the one who should be thanking you—for having me."

Kayla got up, walked over to him and kissed him on the cheek. "I'll let you know when they call."

IT TOOK A MINUTE for Kayla to recognize the white Ford crew cab barreling up the long driveway that afternoon. It was common for neighbors here to visit out of friendliness and curiosity. Several people from town had already dropped by to welcome her and ask how she was fixing to use the land.

"Hi." Ethan opened the truck door. "I thought I'd take a look at how things are going. Hear you got your vines delivered today."

"Welcome to Stony Hill Vineyard," Kayla said, not sure why she felt so pleased to see him, or why she thought he looked so good in a red plaid flannel shirt and a down-filled vest.

He hooked his thumbs in the corners of his jeans pockets. "I don't know anything about vineyards, or wine, for that matter, except I can tell what I like when I taste it."

"That's a good start. White or red?"

"White mostly. But I like a hearty red with a thick, juicy steak, too."

"A man after my own heart." In more ways than one. "Come on, I'll show you around."

She led him to the tin barn they were using as a warehouse. Large, wooden crates were lined up, open, each with dozens of clipped shoots sticking out like porcupine quills. A few showed green nubs ready to burst, but most were still dormant. Her father was in the far corner frowning over the contents of a damaged crate.

"Dad!"

Straightening, he saw their visitor and began walking toward them. At fifty-six he was beginning to develop the rounded shoulders of a man who spent his days bent over. He wasn't overweight, but what he carried was beginning to settle.

"This is Ethan Ritter, our next-door neighbor."

Boyd removed his work gloves and they shook hands. Kayla watched as the two men sized each other up.

"He's here for the grand tour," she said.

"Not a lot to see right now," her father commented. "We just got these in a couple of hours ago. Wait a few months after we get them in the ground, though, and everything greens up. Prettiest sight you ever did see."

Ethan surveyed the rows of oblong boxes, apparently surprised by the large number. "How many...vines do you have here?"

"Six thousand," Boyd said. "Enough for ten acres."

"What kind are they?"

"Chenin blanc."

"Come on," Kayla said. "I'll show you where we'll plant them."

"I've got to get back to work. You two run along." Boyd waved as he returned to the damaged crate. "Nice meeting you, Ethan. Stop by anytime."

"He loves this, doesn't he?" Ethan commented as they stepped out into the bright afternoon sun.

The remark pleased Kayla, perhaps because she also heard approval in it. The two would get along fine, she decided.

She led him to a slope that was out of sight of the house and the road.

Ethan took in the rows of poles and wires as Kayla explained that her father had used the augur on their tractor to make holes in the ground every eight feet.

"Our initial yields won't be very high," she

acknowledged, "and of course we won't know the quality until we taste it, but even poor grapes can be used in blending bulk wines."

"The kind that comes in cardboard boxes." At her shudder, he grinned. "Hey, I told you I'm no connoisseur."

"You're right—" she laughed "—about the market for them, I mean. And that's where our first few harvests will undoubtedly go. As the vines mature, we hope our grapes develop the kind of complexity that'll allow us to bottle under our own label."

"How much can you expect from only ten acres?"

"Between seventy-five and a hundred tons of grapes."

His mouth dropped open. "Did you say 'tons'? How many bottles would that equal?"

"About three thousand cases."

"I'm impressed," he said. "So how'd you get interested in grapes, anyway?"

"Dad's a master winemaker. I grew up in Oregon surrounded by vineyards and majored in viticulture in college."

"Where?"

"University of Washington."

"What are you doing here in Texas? Why not Oregon or Washington or California?"

"Mostly because I had to get Megan away from the cold, damp Northwest." They walked down a row and Ethan tested the tension on the wire trellises. Tight as a bowstring.

"As for California," she went on, "no way could I afford to buy or even lease land there. I considered working for someone else, but the cost of living on the West Coast is beyond my budget. The Home Free program here is a god-send."

"Miranda Wright's brainstorm."

She glanced at him. "You don't approve?"

"On the contrary. The program is brilliant, economically and socially. It'll probably save Homestead."

"Do I hear a *but* at the end of that sentence?"

"The alternative was Clint Gallagher buying up all the land and annexing it to his ranch—the Four Aces. That sure wouldn't have in-creased the population or brought in more tax revenue."

Kayla had the feeling Ethan wasn't telling her everything. She'd heard there'd been a few opponents to the mayor's plan to take posses-sion of a failed ranch, subdivide it and sell off the parcels as a way of bolstering the declin-ing local economy.

"How long does it take to establish a vineyard?" he asked, as they came to the end of the row and turned back.

"It'll be three years before our first harvest. Five to seven years before we know with any certainty what kind of quantity and quality we can produce."

"A pretty long-term capital investment then," he noted. "And a pig in a poke."

"Good investments, like wine and love," she said with a smile, "take time."

He smiled back, and she quickly averted her eyes.

"What're you fixin' to do in the meantime?" he asked.

"Since there aren't any other vineyards around here, I'll probably go for my teaching certificate this summer. I minored in biology in college, and there's usually a demand for science teachers, either full-time or substitute."

They stood at the top of the hill overlooking the barren vineyard. "What kind of irrigation will you use?"

"Drip. Grapevine roots go down rather than laterally, making it ideal as well as ecologically sound."

He nodded, then turned and met her eyes. "If there's anything I can do to help, labor, equipment, manpower...horsepower—" he gave her one of his playful grins "—just let me know. By the way, are we still on for Megan's first lesson this afternoon?"

"Nothing will keep her away. If I don't drive her there, she'll walk. Yep, we're still on."

AFTER HER FIRST riding lesson that afternoon, Megan was convinced she and Birdsong were meant for each other. Ethan wasn't sure it might not be true. The mare had always been patient and imperturbable, except when it came to water. She was the only hydrophobic horse he'd ever encountered. That aside, she was a dream ride with a long, smooth gait. Having been Angela's horse, she was also attuned to the young and infirm, making her ideal for a novice like Megan.

For Megan's second lesson on Wednesday, Ethan had her walk slowly around the arena for ten minutes to warm up. She may have ridden every week for a year, but she hadn't learned much. He suspected it was the fault of the instructor, because the girl was enthusiastic and smart.

From the fence, he continued to repeat instructions on how she should hold the reins and keep her legs straight, heels down. Like most beginners she tended to correct one thing only to lose concentration on another, but she tried so earnestly, he thoroughly enjoyed teaching her.

"My friend, Heather, wishes she could come out and ride with me, too," Megan said as Birdsong walked into a corner and stood there.

"Rein her to the left and nudge her with your feet, like I showed you. That's right."

"Who's Heather?" Kayla asked. She was standing a few feet away on the other side of the fence. The day was exceptionally warm for mid-February, so instead of a jacket, she was wearing a man's flannel shirt. In her snug jeans she was definitely eye-catching, but then she'd look good in anything.

"A girl in my class." Megan grew very serious. "Her mommy and daddy were killed in a car crash, so now she has to live with people she doesn't know."

"Heather Gibbs?" Ethan asked. When Megan nodded, he lowered his voice and explained to Kayla, "She and her parents were coming home from a two-week vacation in Corpus Christi last summer when a van tried to pass them. It blew out a tire and careened into their vehicle. They were pushed into oncoming traffic just as an 18-wheeler was approaching. Heather had been sleeping in the backseat and miraculously survived without a scratch."

"But why is she living with strangers?" Kayla asked.

"As I recall neither parents had siblings, so there was no extended family to take her in." He shook his head. "I didn't realize Heather had ended up in foster care, though. Boy, that's rough. Keep your heels down, Megan," he called out.

After another half hour, he decided his student had ridden long enough. Megan wouldn't admit it but she was getting tired.

"Can I walk her out to the pasture?" she asked after she'd dismounted and was lovingly petting the animal's neck.

"Yep," Ethan said. "Then you have to clean her stall before we bring her in again for supper."

"That's easy. I don't mind, even if it is poop."

He laughed softly and hoped she never lost that enthusiasm. After removing the saddle and replacing the bridle with a halter, they walked Birdsong to the pasture. Once let loose, the mare whinnied to her friends and charged toward them with a kick and a fart, making Megan cup her hands over her mouth and giggle.

"I wonder if Heather's foster parents would let her come out here to ride after school?" he mused, as he and Kayla watched Megan run to the barn.

She shook her head. "I don't imagine they can afford lessons, and I'm sure the state would consider horseback riding a nonreimbursable luxury."

"I don't mean formal lessons, just come out here with Megan and ride around for a while. It's great therapy for troubled kids. I wouldn't charge her."

"That's awfully generous."

He shrugged dismissively. "I have an old gelding she can ride. Fiddlesticks isn't going to run away with anyone."

"Let me make a few phone calls tonight and see what I can set up."

WHEN HEATHER GIBBS arrived with Megan Friday afternoon, Ethan recognized her from a talk he'd given about horses at the elementary school last spring at rodeo time. The same age as Megan, she was an inch or two taller, a pretty brown-haired girl who'd be a real beauty one day.

Ethan remembered her as a bubbly kid who'd raised her hand several times to ask good questions. Now she seemed passive and lethargic, and there was terrible sadness in her blue eyes. No wonder, after what she'd gone through. A happy little girl on vacation with her family one day, a lonely, confused orphan the next.

Ever the leader, Megan dragged her by the hand to meet Ethan. "This is my friend Heather. She's never ridden a horse before."

"Hello, Heather." Ethan extended his hand. "Welcome to the Broken Spoke Ranch."

Unsure of herself, Heather placed her hand like a paw in his. He shook it once, then let it go. She still hadn't said a word. Ethan caught Kayla's eye and the message that passed between them told him she was as troubled by the melancholy child as he was.

"Come on—" he did his best to sound upbeat "—let me show you around."

They all walked over to the fence, where he pointed to the horses in the pasture. He was beginning to name them when Megan took over. He just smiled and listened, impressed by her accurate description of each: Lottie, the one with one white sock; Izzy, who had a star in the middle of her face. She rattled off the names of the paint, the bay, the sorrel and the chestnut.

"Those are the mares," Megan explained, "the girl horses. The boy horses are kept in another pasture so they won't fight over the girls. Come on, I'll show you where they are."

"Since you've never ridden before," Ethan told Heather a little while later, "why don't you watch Megan ride for a few minutes, see what she does. Then if you'd like to ride, too, I'll put you up on Fiddlesticks."

"Birdsong is my horse," Megan informed her. Not for the first time, Ethan suspected.

Kayla sat with Heather on the bench Carter had moved to the side of the arena. Ethan saw Kayla speak to the shy girl from time to time, but as far as he could tell Heather said virtually nothing in return.

After twenty minutes, Ethan told Megan she could ride in the arena by herself, but only at the walk.

He went over to where Heather was sitting. "Would you like to try now?"

She nodded shyly.

"Let's go meet Fiddlesticks, then."

She took the hand he offered and together they went to the hitching post where he'd tied the gelding next to a mounting block. Knowing how intimidating a full-size horse could be to a child, he didn't rush things.

"First, let's get you two acquainted." Still holding her hand, he guided her onto the first step. It was steep and she lost her balance, panicked and clung to his neck.

"I've got you," he assured her.

For a moment she seemed reluctant to let him go. What was running through her mind? Ethan wondered. Had her dad been the kind of man to hold his daughter when she was frightened or tired? Had anyone held her since her parents had disappeared from her life?

"Fiddlesticks, this is Heather," he told the horse. "She'd like to ride you this afternoon." The animal just stood there, of course.

As he had with Megan, he showed Heather how to hold out her hand so the horse could sniff it. "Good as a handshake," he said, and encouraged her to rub the nose. He saw the hint of a smile on her face when she did. The velvety softness of a horse's snout always fascinated the uninitiated.

"Ready?" he asked.

He sensed both her apprehension and excitement when she nodded. Assuring her everything was going to be fine, he lifted her into the saddle. "Seeing as this is your first time, you can hold on to the horn, if you want to."

He walked the twenty-five-year-old gelding—his father's favorite—toward the arena, confident the horse wouldn't spook, especially with a child on his back.

"Looking good, Heather." Kayla smiled up at the girl as she opened the arena gate so they could enter.

Ethan kept the pace slow as he led her first in one direction, then in the other. Fiddlesticks was patient, and Heather began to relax. Not completely, but her initial fear was dissipating.

The girls had just finished and dismounted when Luella appeared with a plate of home-made cookies. She was a small woman, only a little over five feet, and despite her expertise in the kitchen, she was quite slender. Almost sixty, she'd been with the Ritters over thirty years.

"I figured you girls could use a break," she said, "and I thought you might like to try my pecan-butter cookies. They're like peanut-butter cookies, 'cept they're made with pecans, of course."

Ethan reached for one. She slapped his fingers. "Mind your manners. Guests first. Besides, you'll hog them all and nobody else will get a chance to even taste them."

She held out the plate for Kayla and the girls, and Ethan watched Kayla almost melt in front of him as she bit into one. He smiled at Luella, who smiled back.

"Now, if you don't like them," she said, "you just tell me, and I'll fix something else next time."

"Mmm. These are delicious," Kayla said.

"Yummy." Megan took a second.

Ethan watched Heather as she nibbled the edge of hers. All of a sudden tears were streaming down her face. Putting an arm across her shoulder, he didn't have to ask what was bothering her. He just let her cry against his shirt.

KAYLA WAS IMPRESSED with Ethan's skill at handling the traumatized child. He hadn't pushed, as many adults did with children who were withdrawn. He accepted her silence and her tears as perfectly natural. Kayla hadn't missed the way the girl had clung to him when she'd lost her balance or again when he'd helped her onto the horse, either. In those fleeting moments it occurred to Kayla that the girl was reaching out for more than physical support, and to Kayla's amazement, Ethan seemed to understand that.

How had he developed this remarkable rapport with children?

"Did you have a good time today?" she asked as she drove Heather home. Her foster mom was too busy to come and get her. Kayla didn't mind, even if it was fifteen miles round-trip.

"Yes, ma'am," Heather answered softly, as if she wasn't supposed to be there.

"Would you like to come again?"

"Yes, ma'am." Kayla heard a spark of hope in this reply.

She couldn't imagine the depth of loneliness and despair the poor child had endured. She herself had been a toddler when her mother had died in an automobile accident. She had no clear memory of Carol Crawford, just a few snapshots of the pretty young woman Kayla had come to resemble. Her father had been her whole world. She'd often wished he'd remarry so she could have a mother like other children, but he'd never even dated when she was growing up. He'd been a good dad, though; always there when she needed him.

"I'll stop and talk to Mrs. Rayborn and see if you can come to the Broken Spoke with Megan during the week. Okay?"

"Yes, ma'am. Thank you, ma'am."

Had she always been so polite? So compliant? Or had she learned to be this submissive?

The neighborhood Heather lived in wasn't a slum, but it wasn't too far removed from one, either. The houses were old, small and close together. Many of them needed painting. Only a few still had one-car garages. Most of the others had been converted to living space. Cars were parked on the street, under tacked-on carports and, occasionally, on lawns.

"Megan, please stay here while I talk to Mrs. Rayborn. I won't be long."

The woman who answered the door seemed about to yell as she swung it open. She stopped when she saw Kayla and Heather.

"Are you Mrs. Rayborn? I spoke to you yesterday on the phone. I'm Kayla Price. I hope I'm not interrupting anything."

On the other side of forty, Leona Rayborn was a big woman in height and girth. She had an infant propped against her shoulder. A TV blared behind her. How the baby slept through the din was a mystery.

"Oh, hi. Did you have a good time riding, Heather?"

"Yes, ma'am."

"I'm glad. Now go change your clothes, honey, and clean your room."

The girl brushed past her and ran inside.

"And be sure to throw your dirty clothes in the hamper this time," Mrs. Rayborn called after her. "We eat in fifteen minutes."

She turned back to Kayla. "Place is a madhouse this time of day, what with meals and getting the little ones ready for bed. Randy's late again, so it's all on me. Thanks for bringing her home." She was about to close the door when Kayla spoke up.

"If I can just take a minute… Would it be all right to have the school bus drop Heather off at the Broken Spoke with my daughter after school on Mondays, Wednesdays and Fridays? She seems to enjoy riding, and I think it'll be good for her. Megan really enjoys being with her."

"I'm glad she's finally making friends—" Leona shifted the baby to her other shoulder "—but if this is going to cost anything—"

"Not a cent," Kayla assured her. "Mr. Ritter doesn't want any money."

"Monday, Wednesday and Friday, you say. Somebody will have to do her chores on those days."

"Can she trade days with one of the other children?"

The woman thought a minute. "If horseback riding'll get her out of that shell, I guess we can work something out. You'll have to bring her home, though. I can't go running out after her. Enough to do around here with all the others."

"How many children do you have?" Kayla asked.

"Six, including this one. Just got him yesterday. Three months old. The little ones are the most work. Probably shouldn't have taken him, but the poor thing's got no place else to go. Make sure Heather's home by six. That's when we eat."

"If we're late, I'll pick something up for her along the way," Kayla offered.

"That'll be fine. You got a cell phone?"

Kayla nodded.

"I'd appreciate it if you'd call and let me know. And please, not a bunch of junk. I'm having enough trouble getting her to eat properly. I sure don't want her getting sick on me, too."

"I'll be careful. I promise. And thank you, Leona. I know Heather will appreciate it."

"Monday, Wednesday and Friday. Got it. I'll let her know."

"Is she going to be able to come, Mommy?" Megan asked the second Kayla opened the car door.

"Yes, honey. Three days a week."

"Yay!"

Kayla drove away wishing she could do more for the sad little girl.

CHAPTER THREE

ETHAN WAS PLEASED WITH the girls' progress over
the next week. Megan's desire to improve was
starting to shape her albeit undiminished enthusiasm. As for Heather, not only was her riding stronger as she took control of the reins and
used her legs, but she was beginning to open
up, to talk with him and Kayla. Nothing dra-
matic, but there were occasional exchanges that
came close to conversation.

On Friday, as Ethan and Kayla were helping
the girls down from the horses, Heather said
Brad wanted to know if he could come out and
ride, too.

"Who's Brad?"

"He lives with me at the Rayborns'."

Not home, Ethan noted, but *at the Rayborns'*.
"How old is he?"

"Nine, but he's in the same class as me."

"How come?"

"'Cause his father wouldn't let him go to
school. Said he was bad."

"Is that the foster father you're living with?"

"Uh-uh. His last name is Estes. He lives with us because his daddy's in jail. His mommy is, too, or maybe rehab. Leastways, he can't live with her."

"Has he ever been on a horse before?" At that age Ethan was already an accomplished rider.

"Nuh-uh. His daddy wouldn't let him, and now he's afraid nobody will."

"Why's that?" Ethan asked.

"'Cause he's only got one foot."

That stopped him for a moment. "I'm sorry to hear that. Was he born that way?"

Heather shook her head. "When he was six his daddy got mad at him for not standing still, so he nailed his foot to the floor and they had to cut it off."

Ethan wasn't sure he'd heard right. Children sometimes exaggerated or even made things up.

He set her on the ground. "Is that true?"

She looked up and nodded sadly, and Ethan had no doubt she at least believed it was.

While Megan and Heather cleaned their tack and put out the feed Carter had measured for them beforehand, Ethan drew Kayla aside.

"Do you know anything about a boy named Brad Estes?"

"Heather told you about him?"

"Did his father really—"

"Nail his foot to the floor? Yes. He walks with a limp sometimes, and my dear indefatigable daughter, who hasn't yet learned the word *discretion,* asked him why. He showed her his artificial foot and told her how he got it. I was skeptical, too, so I asked some people at church. Apparently his father was on drugs. By the time his mother took the kid to the emergency room, gangrene had set in."

Ethan gritted his teeth and hoped the boy's father didn't get out of jail for a very long time. "Heather says he wants to ride. Could you talk to Mrs. What's-her-name—"

"Rayborn. You want me to see if she'll let him come out, too?"

"Yeah. Speaking of which, how safe is Heather in that foster home?"

"I checked with Child Protective Services. The Rayborns have been taking in kids for about eight years and have a good reputation. I've met Leona. I wouldn't call her one of the warmest people I've ever encountered, but she and her husband, Randy, seem to take good care of the kids they foster."

"Why does 'good' not sound good enough to me?"

"It's not a perfect situation for those children," she agreed, "but some of the alternatives are worse."

He wasn't pacified. "See if Brad can come to ride, too."

THE FIRST THING Ethan noticed when Brad showed up the following Monday with Megan and Heather was that he was small for his age and skinny. He was polite enough and excited about coming out to the ranch, but he was leery, as well. A kid on perpetual guard.

Ethan didn't notice any limp. Maybe Brad only had one when he got tired or hurt himself.

Ethan quickly discovered the boy was also strong. He clamped his knees tightly against the saddle when told to, and he had the natural dexterity and coordination of a decent athlete. His handicap didn't have to restrict him. There were, after all, one-footed football kickers, one-handed baseball players, athletes who had only one eye. Handicaps were regarded as challenges these days, not impediments.

"You have three students now, but only one of them is paying," Kayla said the following Wednesday afternoon when the kids were doing their barn chores, which they seemed to relish. "Doesn't seem very profitable."

"It's also not costing me anything," he pointed out. "Besides, this isn't about money."

The children came running out of the barn, circled a wheelbarrow full of manure and ran back inside. All three were laughing.

"No," she said, "I guess it isn't."

She kept watching him, and he had the feeling she was trying to see inside him.

Don't, he wanted to tell her. *What you find you won't like.*

He strode to the barn, as if he had something important to do. He did—get away. Being close to her made him uncomfortable. He liked the opposite sex. Always had. But he didn't get involved with married women or divorcées with children. Much too complicated. He didn't have anything to offer a woman with responsibilities. He was a good-time sort of guy, nothing more. He'd messed up his own family. He had no intention of messing up anybody else's.

The following Wednesday he was sitting atop Cinco giving the three youngsters a lesson in the big outdoor arena—Megan on Birdsong, Heather on Fiddlesticks and Brad on Joker—when he heard the gurgle of a diesel pulling up the driveway. He swiveled in the saddle but didn't recognize the maroon pickup that stopped next to Kayla's Toyota. Didn't immediately recognize the driver, either. He and Kayla, however, greeted each other familiarly.

The visitor wasn't exceptionally tall even in cowboy boots, but he had the brawny bulk of someone who worked out with weights. After shaking Kayla's hand, he stood behind the fence, gazing out at the children riding inside the oblong arena. It wasn't until he removed his Western hat and brushed back his wheat-colored hair that Ethan recognized him.

Noah. Holden Kelley's son. He'd been on the football team with Ethan's brother, Jud. Ethan knew Noah had taken over as minister of the local church after his father had suffered a second stroke a couple of months ago. A chip off the old block, no doubt.

Turning away from him and Kayla, Ethan asked the children to reverse direction and continue at a walk. After ten minutes, Megan was growing bored with the slow pace—the kid was always on the move. Even Heather seemed anxious to trot, and Brad had enough natural ability, in spite of his size, to handle it.

"Okay, kids, line up at the far end."

They obeyed quickly and eagerly.

"We're going to learn to trot now."

"Yay!" Megan sang out.

Ethan rode around the arena, demonstrating the proper form.

"To trot, you have to squeeze with your legs, let up slightly on the reins, then give the horse a little kick with your heels to make him go faster."

He trotted another full circuit and drew to a halt in front of them.

"You first, Megan. Trot from where you are to the other end of the arena, then slow to a walk and turn around."

He wasn't surprised when she bounced like a puppet with half the strings broken. She didn't fall off, but she came close, and he could see the sheer terror on her face as she clutched the saddle horn. Ethan still couldn't understand how such an eager student hadn't learned to trot in a year of lessons. He shrugged off the thought and found a couple of good points to praise—she'd kept her shoulders back and only lost one stirrup—and gave her several pointers on what she needed to do to improve. Heather's turn.

The first time trotting was scary; he could see doubts and fear clouding her eyes.

"Same thing. One length," he said.

She kicked Fiddlesticks halfheartedly without results.

"Loosen up on the reins a little." When she

did, he clicked his tongue and ordered the horse into a collected trot. Heather grabbed the saddle horn and bounced violently in the saddle. At not quite the halfway point, Ethan called the horse down to a walk.

"That was a real good start," he assured her as she returned to her place. "Next time, tighten your knees more and you'll do even better."

Brad's turn.

"Keep your legs straight and tighten your knees. Ready?"

The boy nodded.

"Now give Joker a kick to get her going."

The look of shock on the boy's face at the first violent bounce was inevitable, but he instinctively clamped his knees. After initially grabbing the horn, he released it and held the reins in front of him. Ethan watched his eyes. The kid was intense, his attention focused exclusively on what he was doing.

He's going to be all right. Instead of one length, Ethan let him trot home.

The girls clapped their hands in approval, surprising Ethan with their generosity. He praised the boy and watched his eyes light up. How long had it been since anyone had given him real encouragement?

While the children resumed riding in a circle—

theoretically cooling their horses down—Ethan nudged Cinco over to the sidelines.

Noah looked up at him, smiling pleasantly. "You're making those kids very happy."

Ethan swung out of the saddle. "They're doing okay."

"I'm Noah Kelley." They shook hands. Noah's grip was firm. "You probably don't remember me. It's been a while—"

"What brings you out here?"

Ethan sensed Kayla stiffen at his abrupt manner. Noah seemed not to notice.

"Kayla was telling me what a terrific job you're doing with these kids, and I thought I'd come out and see for myself."

"I'm not a member of your congregation. You don't have to check up on me."

Noah snorted, seemingly more amused than offended by the remark. "Actually I'm here as an envoy."

"Well, why don't you go ahead and deliver your message." *And leave.*

"Not a message, a request. Some of our congregation have children with special needs. After hearing what Kayla had to say Sunday about the great job you've been doing here with Heather and Brad, they're wondering if you'd be willing to give their kids horseback lessons, as well. They'll be happy to pay you," he added.

"How many kids?"

"Six altogether."

Seven paying students instead of one. The income would certainly be welcome. He'd have to juggle his schedule.... "Why didn't they ask me themselves? Why send you?"

Noah shrugged his muscular shoulders. "They were afraid you'd turn them down, I reckon."

"And they thought you might have special influence?"

Noah flashed his pearly whites. "Pretty naive, huh?"

Out of the corner of his eye, Ethan caught Kayla staring at him. He knew he was acting like a jerk, but Kelley wasn't a name he had reason to respect. "What are their ages and problems?"

Noah reached into a breast pocket and pulled out a piece of paper. "I've written it all down for you. Names, ages, physical or mental impairments, as well as telephone numbers in case you want to talk to their parents or guardians."

"Do they understand that I'm not a therapeutic riding instructor?" Ethan asked. "I have no credentials, no particular training. For all they know, I might be doing their kids more harm than good."

"You obviously have a way with children, Ethan. They respond to you because you genuinely care about them."

"That's a pretty glowing evaluation after just a few minutes of observation."

Noah smiled. "It's not my judgment, Ethan, it's Kayla's. She's been impressed with what you've been able to do with Heather and Brad."

Ethan glanced at her. She nodded a bit tentatively, apparently unsure of his response.

He folded the paper and stuck it in his hip pocket. "I'll think about it."

"Good. If you decide to take on just one or two of them, perhaps as a start, that's fine." Noah extended his hand, forcing Ethan to take it again. "Thanks for hearing me out."

He tipped his hat to Kayla, turned and sauntered back to his truck.

WHEN ETHAN TOLD Kayla Monday afternoon after his lesson with the children that he was calling off Wednesday's session, he offered no explanation, and she didn't ask for one. He was, after all, entitled to a personal life, plus running a horse ranch was probably a lot more complicated than just feeding horses and cleaning stalls, but she was curious.

Her father furnished the answer later that night by handing her the *Homestead Herald*.

"Page two," he said and shuffled off to bed.

The local newspaper was small, only a few folds and seemed to contain the same advertisements for the feed store, the general store, the hardware and drugstore in the same spots every week. Why not? Not likely to find many sales or bargains in a town of fewer than fifteen hundred people. The closest competition was in San Antonio, thirty miles away.

The heart of the paper was local news and gossip. Because the Home Free program was so important to the community, legal notices were also posted—along with the names of the people who were getting land, where their property was located, what the new owners intended to use the land for, and perhaps most importantly, how many children they had. One of the reasons behind the program had been to lure families back to the shrinking town, since its schools were in danger of being closed. Nobody wanted their kids bused miles away to other communities.

The brief article on page two announced that Ethan Ritter had been granted official permission to transfer his father's remains from the public cemetery in Homestead to the family plot on the Broken Spoke, and that the reinterment was scheduled for Wednesday afternoon.

The revelation came as a shock to Kayla. It meant the ranch had previously been owned by the Ritters, undoubtedly for a long time, since there was a family graveyard on it. Yet she was sure she'd been told Ethan was part of the land giveaway program.

Time for research, and who better to ask than Millicent Niebauer, who seemed to know everything about everybody and had few qualms about sharing it.

THE NIEBAUER PRESS, which published the *Homestead Herald,* was a throwback to a bygone era. Its ancient offset printing presses were still in place, too big to be moved. Except as collector's items, they probably weren't worth more than their weight in scrap iron. Nowadays, Millicent Niebauer, a sparrow of a woman, wrote all the articles for the newspaper on a computer, and they were printed in the back by her husband, Hiram. The tall, scrawny man was as taciturn as she was talkative.

Kayla was well aware that her exploratory visit to the paper would require tit for tat. Smiling, she entered the old-fashioned print shop fully prepared.

"Mrs. Price—" Millicent didn't have to pause a heartbeat to remember Kayla's name "—how very nice to see you. I've been hearing all sorts of wonderful things about that vineyard you're planting."

"Please, call me Kayla."

"Heard your daughter is taking riding lessons from Ethan Ritter, too, even though he wouldn't sell you Birdsong. Can't say I'm really surprised, of course."

"He said he couldn't in good conscience sell me a thirty-year-old horse."

Millicent's right brow went up. "Yes, I reckon that's as good an excuse as any."

Kayla was sure there was a specific reason for her choice of words, but she let it pass, confident she'd learn what it was eventually.

"I stopped by, Mrs. Niebauer, to tell you how much I enjoy the *Herald.* You do such a wonderful job making it informative and friendly. I feel like a member of the community just reading it."

The older woman preened. "Why, thank you, dear, and call me Millie. Everybody does. We don't have a big paper, but I do my best with it."

"It shows. It's really good. I noticed Ethan's

going to be moving his dad's remains to the Broken Spoke. Is that common here in Texas, to bury family members on private property?"

"Oh, my, no. You have to obtain special permission from the state, but the Broken Spoke was in the Ritter family for well over a hundred years. His mama and sister are buried there, you know, along with other members of the family."

Kayla was confused. "But I thought he just bought the place in the same land deal I did."

"Well, yes, that's true, but his family owned it before that."

Kayla tilted her head. "I don't understand."

Millie smiled, please to be the source of fresh information. "I forget that everybody doesn't know the history. Well, it started a dozen years ago now, when the K-bar-C went into bankruptcy after Clyde Braxton died. He was in his eighties by then and having a hard time keeping the place going. His children, the ungrateful lot…well, they weren't any help. Spent money like it was going out of style. After he died, it did, too. Served them right, if you ask me, but it's not for me to judge."

She rearranged the announcement cards on the long counter between them, cards that had been on display for some time, considering the way they were yellowing around the edges.

"Anyway," she continued, "when the place came up for sale at auction a bunch of the local ranchers decided to pool their resources and buy it. Ethan's daddy, Zeb, merged the Broken Spoke into KC Enterprises, as they called their consortium, and, since his place was more or less in the middle of it all, he became the foreman. Did a good job, too, but times were against them."

She went over to the end of the counter, poured coffee into two ceramic mugs emblazoned with Don't Mess With Texas and handed Kayla one. "Don't know how much you know about ranching—"

"Very little, I'm afraid," Kayla conceded. And as Ethan had pointed out, nothing about horses.

"Well, it's a hard life, despite all the glamour them fools out in Hollywood make it look like. Hard on men and harder on the women, if you ask me. There's no oil around here, as you might have noticed, so you have to work for what you get."

She sipped her coffee and made a face. "Reckon I need to make a fresh pot."

She shoved the two cups aside, went to a

small refrigerator behind a filing cabinet and brought over two soft drinks.

"These are the real Dr Pepper," she said proudly. "Was up in Dallas last week and stopped off in Dublin. That's the only plant still bottling the original recipe, using cane sugar instead of corn sweeteners." She took a slug, smacked her lips and set the bottle on the counter.

"Things went fine for a couple of years," she continued. "Like I said, old Zeb knew his stuff. Trouble is, the drought hit and they found themselves overextended. The bank refused them any more credit."

She leaned closer, as if anyone else were around. "Mind you, I don't know if it's true, but they say Clint Gallagher blocked them loans."

"The state senator?"

"Can't prove it, of course, and wouldn't dare print a word of it, but that's what some folks say. Anyway, KC Enterprises went bottom up two years ago. You would've expected the place to go on the auction block again, but Miranda convinced the city council to foreclose for taxes and take it over."

"And that's the land being given away now," Kayla concluded.

"Yep. Old Clint wasn't too happy about it, I

can tell you. Probably figured he had a right to pick the spread up for a song and back taxes and add it to his empire."

"So what happened to Ethan's father?"

"Lost the Broken Spoke when KC Enterprises went bust. By then his wife and daughter had passed on. His oldest son, Jud, had moved off to greener pastures years before. Zeb and Ethan leased a dinky little place on the edge of town. Ethan worked real hard to make a go of it, buying and selling horses, training them. But it was all too much for Zeb. He started drinking pretty heavy. Last year he committed suicide. Shot himself. Ethan's the one that found him."

Losing a loved one was hard enough. Finding him dead had to be even worse. But suicide! Survivors were inevitably plagued by self-doubt, forever wondering what they should have done to prevent it.

"Ethan wanted his daddy to be buried on the ranch with his other kin, but the family no longer had legal claim to the land, so his request was denied. I reckon that's why he chose that particular parcel to buy. He grew up in that house, you know. A lot of memories on that land, and of course the graveyard where his ma and sister are buried."

"It's a sad story," Kayla said.

Millicent nodded. "I hope laying his daddy to rest there will bring them both some peace."

ETHAN'S NIGHT WAS filled with memories, mostly sad. Even the few that were happy were clouded by melancholy foreshadowing.

If only I'd been able to get you to hang on a little while longer, Dad. Ethan lay in the shadowy darkness of his old room. *I've gotten our house back and at least a little of the land. The stable's doing real well now, too, making a decent profit, even after I gave Carter and Luella a pay raise. They're happy to be home, too.*

Now, with the Broken Spoke homeplace back, he had the facilities to board a dozen horses in addition to his own. In fact he had a waiting list of people who wanted to keep their horses there. He was starting to turn a nice profit buying and selling horses, too. In another year or so he figured he'd be able to build another barn, one that was bigger and better.

He rose as dawn was coloring the sky pink and found Luella already sitting at the kitchen table, a cup of coffee clasped between her work-worn hands. More unusual was Carter being there, as well. The old man took his noon and evening meals with them, but he tended to keep to himself in the morning. Ethan doubted they'd slept much the night before, either.

Today would be as difficult for these two people as it would be for him. He poured himself a cup of the hot, bitter brew and joined them.

"Crew'll be here at ten to dig the grave," he announced. "Casket at two."

A small grunt from Carter was the only response.

After a few minutes, Luella asked, "You let Jud know?"

Ethan had thought about contacting his brother, but Jud hadn't come home after their father died last year, so this second burial wouldn't mean anything to him, either.

To be fair, Jud had been in the hospital in Austin recovering from an injury when he got the word of their father's death, but he could have come home later. Ethan tried not to resent his brother for staying away. Maybe he was even grateful he hadn't shown up. He didn't need to see the accusation in his brother's eyes to feel another stab of guilt.

"No," he said.

Neither made any comment.

"There was a notice in the *Herald*," Luella

said a few minutes later. "People will want to pay their respects."

Ethan shook his head. "I wish Millie would mind her own business."

Carter grunted. "Her old man would go broke if she did. Only reason anybody reads that rag is for the gossip. The CIA could take pointers from her on confidential sources."

It was a long speech and one with a rare note of humor for Carter. In spite of himself, Ethan laughed.

The next hours were filled with routine chores, which should have made the time fly by, but it didn't. It dragged.

He and Carter fed and watered the horses, then put them out to graze. Ethan mucked out stalls, spread the manure in a pasture where it would fertilize and soften the footing. He replaced fluorescent tubes in the overhead lights in several of the stalls and repaired a worn hinge that would soon need replacing, then he worked with a green three-year-old for nearly an hour.

Finally the workmen arrived. Ethan led them to the spot, a narrow space beside his mother, Valerie, and sister, Angela, one row forward of his grandparents and great-grandparents. He'd straightened up the tombstones when he'd reclaimed the land—a mere forty acres out of the thousand-plus they'd once owned. A pittance by Texas standards, but it would have to be enough. At least he'd gotten the barns and house—what had once been home. The rest was just land, or so he tried to tell himself. This was where his family had lived, and for over a hundred years, thrived.

The operator of the backhoe was an expert. He carved out a neat rectangular hole without disturbing anything around it. They inserted the concrete liner that the law now required, then the machinery was pulled discreetly out of sight. Ethan had already purchased a new headstone, one that matched the style of the others. Tradition.

There wouldn't be any more Ritters, not from him and, as far as he could tell, not from his brother. His sister had never even gone to a dance or had a date, much less kissed a boy behind the barn....

After supervising the grave digging, Ethan wandered over to the bunkhouse. He'd offered Carter one of the bedrooms in the big house, but the lifelong bachelor preferred his privacy. He'd selected the foreman's room in the empty dormitory, across from the plain, utilitarian kitchen the hired help had used in the days when they had a full crew on the place. He kept soda and beer in an ancient refrigerator out here, along with a few snacks.

The old ranch hand was sitting at the scrubbed wood table, a half-empty bottle of bourbon in front of him, a couple of fingers of it in a jelly glass.

"Early start?" Ethan asked.

Carter wasn't much of a drinker, and if Ethan hadn't known the bottle was nearly half-gone to begin with, he might have been worried.

Carter grunted but didn't make a move to touch the whiskey.

Ethan wasn't much of a drinker, either, but there were times when it seemed appropriate. He grabbed another jelly glass off a shelf and splashed a half ounce of the amber liquid into it.

Carter picked up his drink. "Welcome home, Zeb." He tossed it off, slammed down the glass and stomped through the screen door, letting it bang behind him.

Ethan took a deep breath. "Yeah, welcome home, Dad."

He coughed after downing the shot, washed both glasses, put the bottle away, then filled a taller glass with orange juice to get the taste of death out of his mouth.

CHAPTER FOUR

BY ANNOUNCING THE TIME of Zeb Ritter's interment at the Broken Spoke in the *Herald,* Millie Niebauer had essentially invited people to attend. Kayla wanted to pay her respects, as well, but that presented a dilemma. Taking Megan wasn't a problem, but Kayla hadn't canceled Heather and Brad's school bus drop-off. Not knowing the reason Ethan had called off the riding class, she'd figured the three kids could pass the time together playing at Stony Hill. That Heather and Brad would welcome the break from their large foster family.

But she couldn't very well leave them home alone while she went over to the Broken Spoke. It seemed cruel to take Heather to a burial so soon after her own parents had died.

"Leave them all here with me," her father had suggested at lunchtime when she brought up the subject. "There's plenty around here to keep them interested."

"You don't mind?"

"Of course not. You know how I love to show off."

Kayla had to smile. He did have something of the pedant in him, but he was also a good teacher. The plan fell apart, however, the moment the kids got off the bus.

"Mommy, why aren't we having a riding lesson with Ethan today?"

"He's busy with other things, honey. Grandpa's hoping the three of you can give him a hand in the vineyard. Bet you never planted grapevines," she said to Brad.

"Aren't you going to be here?" Megan asked.

"In a little while. I have to run over to Ethan's for a few minutes, then I'll be right back."

"Why are you going over there if Ethan is busy, Mommy?"

She should have said she had an errand to do in town, but Kayla didn't like lying to her daughter, even for her own good. Besides, in her experience lies backfired and made matters worse. Equivocating rarely got her anywhere, either, not with her precocious daughter. The children gazed at her, clearly expecting a better explanation than the one she'd just fumbled. She had no choice but to explain.

"Ethan's father died last year. He was buried in the cemetery on the other side of town. You remember, we saw it when we were driving to San Antonio to see the Alamo."

"That's where Davy Crockett was killed," Megan stated.

"Yes, it is. Well, there's also a cemetery on the Broken Spoke, and Ethan is having his father buried there today."

"They dug him up?" Brad asked with the fascination boys seem to have with the macabre.

Kayla shook her head and wished she'd prepared a convincing lie beforehand. "They're moving the casket, the box he's in."

"They won't open it, will they?" Heather asked.

"No, no. All anyone will see is the casket."

"Can we go, too?" Megan asked.

"I won't be long and Grandpa—"

"I want to go," Megan insisted.

"It wouldn't be polite to leave your friends here."

"I'd like to go, too," Brad announced. "I've never seen a casket, 'cept in movies."

Kayla glanced at Heather, trying to gauge her reaction.

"I'll go," the girl said.

Kayla shook her head. "It'll be better if you all stay here. I won't be long, then we can play some games, and I'll fix a special supper. Do you like fried chicken? I've got a really good recipe. Megan will tell you how good it is."

"People came to see my mommy's and daddy's caskets," Heather said. "I didn't know all of them. The people I did know told me they were sorry."

A lump formed in Kayla's throat. "You can tell Ethan you're sorry when you see him next time," she said, amazed the words didn't come out strangled.

"I'd like to tell him today. I don't mind seeing a casket."

This wasn't turning out the way Kayla had anticipated or wanted.

"Are you sure?" She hoped the girl would change her mind. "You really don't have to. It's all right to offer your condolences on Friday when you have your riding lesson."

"Ethan's my friend," Heather replied with more determination than Kayla would have expected.

Boyd came to the rescue. "Why don't we all go, then we can come back here and play dominoes. Have either of you ever played Mexican Train?"

And so the five of them piled into Kayla's Toyota. She wondered if she was doing the right thing. Would attending this burial further traumatize the girl? On the other hand, children were more resilient than adults often gave them credit for, and Heather seemed to understand what was going on.

"If we get a chance to talk to Ethan—" she turned onto the ranch road "—all you have to say is 'I'm sorry for your loss,' or 'I'm sorry about your father.' We'll stay only long enough to let him know we're his friends. Okay?"

She heard a muted chorus of okays from the backseat.

Kayla was surprised at the number of vehicles parked around the arena. Noah's maroon pickup was among them.

They didn't have any trouble finding the gravesite. It was on the hill behind the house, past a grove of oak trees.

She recognized some of the people gathered there. The town's mayor. Tall and statuesque, Miranda seemed to be perpetually on the move. Even now, as she spoke quietly to Noah, she seemed ready to bolt.

Millicent Niebauer was there, of course, taking it all in.

Frances Haase, the town librarian, was almost as tall as Miranda, but narrow and angular in build. Kayla knew the fiftyish woman was on the town council and the Home Free land giveaway board.

She was surprised to see Arlen Enfield here. He'd been the mayor before Miranda, and from what Kayla had heard, he'd been a strong opponent of the Home Free program. On the one occasion Kayla had chanced to meet him in town, he'd come across as polite, sophisticated and charming—the consummate politician.

Beside him was Wade Montgomery, the local sheriff. He was standing with an older man— based on their looks, it must be a relative. His father, probably. Kayla searched for a name. Jock. He'd been one of the partners with Zeb in KC Enterprises.

Less than a minute after they found places on the periphery of the small group, Noah Kelley took a position at the head of the shiny mahogany casket suspended over the open grave.

Ethan stood on one side of it with Carter Dunlap and Luella Hernandez.

"Thank you all for coming," Noah said, "to pay our last respects to Zeb Ritter, a member of our community."

Ten minutes later the service was over. Those in attendance came around the head of the grave to shake Ethan's hand and offer their condolences. Megan followed her grandfather, the other children behind her.

"I'm sorry about your father," she said, just as she'd been instructed. Kayla felt relief until the girl added, "How come he died? Was he sick? My Grandma Price got sick and died, too."

"I'm sorry to hear that." Ethan sent Kayla a sharp glance.

"So did your daddy get sick, too?" Megan persisted.

"Megan, move on, please," Kayla said quietly but forcefully, "so Heather and Brad can offer their condolences."

Not nearly as chatty as Megan, Heather stepped forward and held out her hand. "I'm sorry about your daddy, but he's in heaven now with mine."

Kayla watched the muscles in Ethan's jaw tighten before he said, "Yes, he is."

Brad simply shook his hand and mumbled, "Sorry."

Finally, it was Kayla's turn. She held out her hands to him, as well. "I'm very sorry."

He only glared at her. "Why did you bring them here? This is no place—"

"They insisted."

"You should have said no."

"The children have offered to show me around," her father told Ethan. "Is that all right?"

"What? Oh, sure. Luella has cake and cookies at the house when you're finished."

Boyd smiled. "Terrific cookies, too, from what I hear. We won't be long," he added to Kayla.

Ethan returned his attention to Kayla, then abruptly looked past her. "Wait here."

Bewildered by the virtual order, she started to reply but he was already rushing off.

"Noah," Ethan called out. "Hold up."

The minister turned and waited.

"Thank you for coming." He slowed, stopped, not sure how to go on. This was the first time he'd ever seen the man in ministerial garb. "Why did you...come today?"

"Because it was the right thing to do, and maybe because I wanted you to know I'm not my father."

Ethan let out a pent-up breath. "I guess you aren't. I owe you an apology. I painted you with the same brush."

Noah nodded sympathetically. "In your place I probably would have, too. You didn't really know me back in high school, but Jud can tell you Dad and I didn't see eye to eye on a lot of things."

"I appreciate your coming today, but you may be in trouble with the elders when they find out you gave a Christian burial to a suicide after your father refused to."

"Last time I checked, we were supposed to pray for the sinner, not the saint. Your father was a good man, Ethan. Don't ever doubt that."

Unexpectedly touched, Ethan offered his hand. This time when they shook the clasp was sincere and hearty. "Won't you come back to the house and have some of Luella's baking?"

Noah looked toward the house and the people spilling out onto the front porch with paper plates in their hands. "Wish I could. She still make those pecan cookies?"

Ethan grinned. "Yep, and they're good as ever."

"Maybe next time." Noah sounded regretful. "But I really have to go. An appointment in town."

They walked to Noah's pickup.

"Have you made any decision about the special-needs kids?"

Ethan nodded. "I've been doing research online. It's a big job, a lot more complicated than just putting them on horses and leading them around in circles. I'm willing to do my part, but I can't do it all myself. I'd like Kayla to help."

"Have you spoken to her about it yet?"

"No, but I'm about to."

"If you need any more volunteers, let me know."

They reached the Chevy. Noah pulled off his clerical garb and tossed it onto the passenger seat, climbed inside and twisted the key in the steering column.

While he waited for the diesel glow-plug signal to go out, he said, "I'm glad you were able to bring your dad home." He nodded toward the children eagerly leading Boyd Crawford from the horse barn to the house, no doubt in search of cookies. "They're lucky to have you, too. If there's anything I can do to help…"

He turned the key. The diesel started up and rumbled noisily. With a wave, he drove off.

WHILE THE KIDS were showing her father all the fascinating things in the barn, Kayla threaded her way through the small, iron-fenced graveyard. The oldest headstones dated back to the mid-nineteenth century and were so weathered they were almost indecipherable. Kayla assumed the woman buried beside Zeb's new grave, Valerie Ritter, was Ethan's mother. She'd died less than four years ago. The fourteen-year-old girl must be his sister. She'd passed away a year earlier.

Kayla noted, too, the months of their deaths. Angela had died in April. So had Zeb—within a few days of the fourth anniversary of his daughter's death. Valerie had died in May.

It was now early March. Spring was about to burst forth with new life. This should be a time of renewal, of joy and promise.

Kayla wandered down to the barn area. As she approached, she could hear the indistinct chatter of the children as they undoubtedly rhapsodized about the horses, the saddles and tack, riding, even cleaning stalls. The solemnity of the past half hour forgotten, as it should be. Leaning against the pipe fence, she scanned the pastures dotted with small clusters of live oaks. The land was green, the sky a cerulean blue, so deep she felt as if she could reach up and touch it. A lone puffy white cloud drifted across the distant horizon.

She sensed Ethan's approach, welcomed it in spite of what she knew was coming. He was unhappy with her, and she understood why. Children shouldn't know death, as participants or spectators.

He came up beside her and rested his elbows

on the fence. Without looking, she was aware of his strength, the broad expanse of his shoulders. The image was as clear in her mind as if she were facing him.

"You shouldn't have brought them."

"They wanted to come, Ethan. Even Heather. I tried to discourage her, but she said you were her friend and she wanted to be here for you."

When he didn't respond, Kayla glimpsed him clenching his jaw as he stared ahead.

"She's grieving, struggling to come to terms with what happened. You've connected with her, Ethan. She feels close to you, maybe closer now because you share a loss."

"Don't make me out a saint, Kayla." His low words were filled with reproach and remorse.

She touched his back. "Not a saint, Ethan, just a man. That's enough." A minute passed in silence. "Noah couldn't stay?"

He exhaled. "He has an appointment in town. He asked me about the riding program for the special-needs kids."

"What did you tell him?"

He looked over at her, a subtle smile on his face. "Be careful what you ask for."

"What?"

"You wanted me to work with handicapped kids, to offer therapeutic riding." The smile grew into a grin. "I told him I'd do it if you were my assistant."

"But...I don't know anything about therapeutic riding."

"Then I guess we're going to have to learn about it together."

Spending hours with this man wasn't a good idea. She had a family, a new vineyard to attend to. "Ethan, I don't have the time," she said, panicking.

"Neither do I."

"But..." There must be some way to get out of this. He was the horseman, the person who had the animals, the riding experience, a talent for teaching.

"So what do you want to do?" he asked. "Tell the kids no, sorry, haven't got the time? Or find it?"

He had her cornered and he knew it. Worse, he seemed to be taking enormous satisfaction in watching her squirm. Did he understand the nature of the predicament he was placing her in, that she was afraid of him, afraid of what being with him would cost her?

"You don't leave me much choice, do you?" she asked with a kind of dread.

"About as much as you left me."

NOBODY STAYED longer than good manners required. After all, this was the second time Zeb had been buried. Kayla, her father and the kids had left hours ago, too. Ethan had given Heather a big hug just before she got into the car.

Luella had overprepared, but he reckoned she'd done that on purpose. The cookies wouldn't go to waste. She'd sent one of her banana-nut loaves home with Kayla, along with the lemon meringue pie she'd noticed Boyd drooling over.

Ethan and Carter were now sitting on the bunkhouse porch drinking coffee.

"Do you know what you're doing?" Carter asked after a sip.

"About what?" Ethan asked innocently.

"You know what I'm talking about. Those kids. Her."

"Noah asked me—"

Carter waved his excuse away with a swing of his mug, sloshing the coffee dangerously close to the rim. "Don't try to bull me, too. I've been around too long to buy it. I saw you the day you was born, and except when you went off to college, I've seen you just about every day of your life since. So quit stallin'. This ain't about Noah. It's about her and the kid."

Ethan suspected he spoke more out of worry than anger.

"I haven't liked all the decisions you've made," the old man went on, "but I've supported them because they were right, and I've respected you for them. I wish what happened hadn't have, but it wasn't your fault. You were as much a victim as she was, but you're screwing up this time."

Ethan held his tongue.

"She's falling in love with you. What then? Leave her the way you have all the others? At least they knew up front what to expect. What happens when this one wants more? You know she will. She's not the kind of gal you pick up at a beer joint."

Maybe that's what I find so attractive. She's somebody, not anybody.

"You've never broken a heart before, far as I know," Carter continued. "But you're going to break hers."

Ethan remained silent.

"You've been spending too much time here with horses," Carter observed. "Your hormones are out of whack. Haul yourself into town and work off some of that energy on the dance floor with some sweet young thing. Maybe then your brain will start working right again."

Ethan laughed. "That's the first thing you've said that makes sense, old man."

It was true. He hadn't been out with a woman since…well, in quite a while. Maybe that was what was driving him so crazy when he was with Kayla—or thinking about being with her. His hormones were out of whack.

He went back to the house, showered, put on freshly pressed jeans and a clean Western shirt and hightailed it into town.

The Saddle Up was technically outside city limits, though the boundary was less than twenty feet east of the parking lot. To the west was Louie's Liquors, which offered a fine selection of beers and wines in addition to the standard variety of distilled spirits.

Happy hour was still underway when Ethan arrived. He bought a longneck for a buck and scoped out the joint. The jukebox was playing right now. The band would start at nine, when the cheap drinks ended.

A hand slapped him on the back. He turned to find Chad Duggan, a guy he'd gone to high school with. Duggan had been a fullback, good enough to be picked up for a college team. He'd blown the opportunity, though, when he tested positive for drugs in his first season. Never did finish college, ended up in rehab a couple of times, got married twice and divorced as often.

"Ain't seen you in a long time. How're the horses?"

"Doing fine. Keeping me busy." Ethan almost asked the next logical question: "What are you up to these days?" But he was leery of the answer. If Duggan was between jobs, which was as likely as not, he'd probably ask if Ethan had any openings at the Broken Spoke. With Carter slowing down and business picking up, Ethan was considering putting on part-time help. Not Duggan, though. And he preferred not to be put in the position of having to turn the guy down. Fortunately he saw someone much more interesting on the other side of the room.

Stacy Holbrook had been the homecoming queen in Ethan's senior year—she was Stacy Hronec then—and they'd dated a few times. She'd married Mitch Holbrook right out of college, but he'd been killed in a small plane crash in Alaska a few months later. A year after that she'd remarried and quickly divorced. Since then she spent a good deal of her free time drinking and dancing.

She greeted Ethan with an open smile. "Well, howdy, stranger."

Someone pulled the plug on the jukebox in

the middle of a tear-jerking ballad, and the band started tuning up. Within a few seconds of striking the first solid chord, the dance floor was packed.

"Still know how to dance?"

He laughed. "I sure hope so."

She was wearing tight jeans and a T-shirt that clung provocatively to her curves.

"You may have to refresh my memory, though."

She grinned. "It'll be my pleasure."

Over the next few hours they paused only when the band did. His first beer got warm before he had a chance to drink it. The second was knocked over. He ordered a third at last call, but by then his mind was on other things.

When the band finally stopped playing, he and Stacy were standing in the middle of the dance floor.

"It's time to go, darlin'," she whispered in his ear. "You are going to be a gentleman and see me home, aren't you? My place isn't real far." She draped her arms over his shoulders. "We can unwind there."

"Sounds inviting." He threw an extra tip on the table, slipped his arm across her back as he escorted her to the parking lot.

"Just follow my taillights," she said breathlessly, when she pulled away to get into her pickup.

"Baby, I promise you. I won't let them out of my sight."

Her eyes glittered. She started her engine. He jogged to his truck, pulled up behind her and flashed his lights.

She lived a mile or so down the road, but the silence of the cab, compared with the blood-pounding beat in the bar, gave him a chance to think, and the cool night air through the open window cleared his head.

He saw Kayla's face. Pictured her standing at the fence, watching the horses and children. He thought about what it might feel like to be with her. To be near enough to catch her scent. To hear her laugh at one of the kids' antics. He tried to imagine what it would be like to hold her.

Stacy pulled into her driveway and switched off her lights. Ethan came to a stop behind her, but left his engine running.

She walked back and stood below his door. "Here we are."

She was warm and willing and eager to please, but this woman's face, this woman's voice, this woman's touch weren't the ones he craved.

"I can't stay," he muttered.

"What?" She gaped at him in shock, then anger.

He didn't blame her. He'd led her on, inferred a promise he couldn't deliver. "I'm sorry."

"What's going on, Ethan?"

"I'm sorry," he repeated. "I have to go."

She stood there with her hands on her hips as he backed out of the driveway. She was still there when he turned and headed for home.

KAYLA WAS COMING in from the vineyard, stretching her tired back muscles when the phone rang. She and her father had elected to do all the planting themselves, both to save money and because they wanted it done right. It would take them about a week, provided their backs didn't give out first. She lifted the receiver.

"Hello, Kayla." Millie at the *Herald*. "Just checking to see if you got any rain last night."

"Rain, no. As far as I know the sky was clear all night."

"Well, we received a trace here in town, thought you might have gotten more. Every drop is a blessing here, you know. Different from where you're from, I reckon."

Kayla laughed. "A bit," she agreed, suspicious that the woman wasn't really calling about the weather.

"Seen Ethan today?"

"No, don't usually go over there on Thursdays. Why?"

"Oh," the newspaper editor drawled, "just wondered how his hangover was."

"Hangover?"

"Well, I heard he closed the Saddle Up last night. Didn't leave with Stacy Holbrook till after one. My sources tell me he was really rocking. Always was a good dancer, even as a teenager."

"Who's Stacy Holcomb?"

"Holbrook," Millie corrected her. "They were sweethearts back in high school. A widow now, well, that and a divorcée. First husband died. Second one ran off. No wonder she spends most of her nights picking up guys."

Kayla was speechless. Regardless, Millie made small talk for another five minutes before finally hanging up.

If there was ever a reason to stay away from Ethan, this was it.

The problem, of course, was that she had to work closely with him if they were going to help the special-needs kids.

CHAPTER FIVE

ON FRIDAY AFTERNOON, WHILE Megan and her friends were cleaning stalls, Ethan drew Kayla outside into the warm spring sunshine to talk about their therapeutic riding program.

"I suggest we evaluate one handicapped child at a time after Megan's riding lesson with Heather and Brad. That means it'll take two weeks to check out all six."

"Can our kids help out?"

Our kids. The words came out of her mouth so naturally she probably hadn't even realized she'd said them.

"Having peers around, encouraging them might give them a sense of security and confidence."

They selected as their first "client" a six-year-old girl with cerebral palsy. Ethan called Noah that evening and told him of their plans. Noah promised that Daphne Jones would be there with her mother promptly at four o'clock Monday.

Ethan spent the weekend working with a new horse that had arrived the previous Thursday. Authorities had removed the young gelding from its owner because of abuse. As a result the animal was skittish around people, especially men.

Ethan placed him in a small corral on the far side of the barn where he had room to pace, yet was still in a controlled environment.

Gaining the confidence of a young horse, especially one that had been mistreated, could be a slow and painstaking process. Ethan spent an hour or two each day with Duke in at least two separate sessions. Upon getting a positive response to an overture, he backed off, essentially rewarding it for good behavior. Sometimes that amounted to no more than crouching in the middle of the corral and watching the animal for minutes on end until its natural curiosity brought it over. Once Ethan was able to touch it in a nonthreatening way without the horse bolting, he let it go.

"That one's slow," Carter said Sunday evening, as Ethan climbed out of the arena through the steel fence.

"He'll be all right. So far it's been one step forward, one step back, but in a few days the two of us will make a giant leap. By the end of the week I'll have a saddle on him, and by the end of next week I'll be riding him."

"You sure about that?" the ranch hand asked, but Ethan knew Carter believed him.

That evening he read up on cerebral palsy. On Monday Kayla came over to the Broken Spoke an hour before the school bus was scheduled to drop the kids off. Her auburn hair burnished by the afternoon sun, she looked absolutely beautiful, though she appeared to be stiff.

"How's the planting going?"

"Almost done." She rolled her shoulders. "Thankfully. I don't know which aches more, my shoulders or my knees."

"Turn around."

"What?"

"Let me see if I can work some of the kinks out."

He stood behind her and placed his hands on her shoulders, then began a slow kneading massage.

"Ah…" She moaned. "I'll give you three hours to stop that. Oh, yes!" She sighed as he dug his thumbs into the tight muscles, rolling her shoulders to accommodate him. "Make that four hours."

He chuckled, enjoying the feel of her under his hands, at the same time trying not to acknowledge the temptation to bend and kiss the nape of her neck.

"How do you want to do this today?" she asked, as she slowly rocked her head back and forth.

"For this initial session Daphne and I will ride Ginger bareback. I'll put her in front of me. That'll give her a sense of security if she has balance problems, and I'll be able to gauge her reactions better." He could feel Kayla starting to relax under his hands. "From what I read, people with cerebral palsy tend to tire easily, so one or two circuits around the arena may be all she can handle this first time. I'll leave it up to her."

Kayla bowed her head, straining against the kinks. "I talked to Daphne and her parents yesterday. She's really excited about coming here. I'm not sure her father is, though. He struck me as very protective." She leaned into Ethan's hands as he rubbed her tired muscles harder. "He kept making noises about putting it off until he could be here, even though his wife insisted she could handle it. Oh, that feels so good." After another moment she added, "I suspect Daphne may be better off not having him around, at least this time."

"Good dads are very protective of their girls," Ethan said casually.

"They'll be here—" Kayla looked at her watch "—in about an hour."

Just then they heard the chatter of kids. Reluctantly Ethan gave Kayla's shoulders one last squeeze. Before releasing her he bent close to her ear. "You still have two and a half hours' credit."

She turned, stretched up and planted a soft kiss on his cheek. "Three and a half. I raised the ante, remember?"

He looked stunned but quickly recovered. "So noted," he said and grinned.

A second later Megan and her friends came charging straight toward them with enthusiastic greetings.

"Hurry and saddle your horses," Ethan instructed them. "Our special guests will be here in an hour. You can clean stalls after they leave."

Forty-five minutes later, while the kids were trotting figure eights across the arena, Ethan put the bareback pad on Ginger, a small palomino. He rode the mare around for a few minutes with the children to warm her up, then he had the kids dismount, unsaddle their horses and turn them out to graze.

On the dot of four, a van pulled slowly up the driveway. Everybody waited. A full three minutes elapsed before a woman emerged from the driver's side, circled the back of the vehicle, removed an aluminum-frame walker and helped her passenger out.

Dark like her mother, the child had short pigtails with bright colored beads at the ends. She appeared undersized for her six years, thin and wiry, but even from a distance Ethan could see the excitement in her black eyes. She moved stiffly, swiveling her hips rather than flexing her legs, which weren't quite fully extended. Her pace was ungainly, but she was determined. A smile lit her face as she approached the arena, her attention pinned on the horse tied up at a rail.

Megan led the welcoming committee, greeting Daphne like an old friend.

"You'll really, really like riding. It's fun," she told the younger girl.

Introductions were made.

"I appreciate you doing this," Shawna Jones told Ethan, her eyes a bit glassy.

It took Daphne some time to make her way to the palomino. Ethan introduced her to the horse, coaxing Ginger into a position so Daphne could rub her nose. The girl was reticent at first, but as Ethan knew would happen, the first touch was enough to fascinate the child. She giggled.

Ethan lifted her onto the mounting block, then jumped up himself. While Shawna helped her daughter balance, he swung his leg over the patient animal and moved slightly back toward the horse's rump. Because Daphne's legs were stiff and parting them was unnatural for her, Ethan and Shawna were very careful to take their time settling her.

Ethan came to appreciate the mother's considerable strength as he gently lowered her daughter over the horse's withers. With Daphne at last in place, he circled his arm around her.

"All right so far?" he asked.

Her nod was jerky. "Yes."

"We're just going to walk today, nice and easy. If it hurts or you get scared, you tell me, okay? You're perfectly safe, Daphne. I'll be holding you the entire time. Ginger is a very gentle horse, so you don't have to worry. I have you. Nothing is going to happen."

"Okay," she whispered.

"Here we go." He nudged the mare into a slow walk. Daphne tensed.

They began a wide circle. Halfway through it Ethan could feel the girl's rigid body start to relax. "You doing all right?"

She nodded. He wished he could see her face.

They continued around a second circle, her mother encouraging her from the sidelines. When Daphne settled against his chest, Ethan wasn't sure if it was from relaxation or exhaustion. His research had indicated fatigue could develop incredibly fast.

As they walked, he was able to see the two women standing on the side with the other children. Shawna was biting her lips, her eyes dark pools.

The mare moved lethargically but steadily, as if she understood the importance of what she was doing.

They completed the second circuit. "Do you want to go around again?" he asked.

"Yes, please."

That made him smile. He urged the horse into a third lap. Toward the end he definitely sensed fatigue in the little girl's posture and called to Kayla to open the gate. He exited the arena and rode up to the mounting block.

"How was it?" he asked.

"It was fun." He could hear her pleasure.

"I knew you'd like riding," Megan chirped. "It's really awesome. And Ginger is a pretty horse. I really like palominos, don't you?"

Shawna was waiting beside the platform.

Ethan leaned back, taking Daphne with him. On opposite sides of the horse, her mother and Kayla lifted the child's legs in unison. Ethan swung her to the left and carefully lowered her, while from the ground Shawna buttressed her daughter's descent. Once Daphne was on her feet and standing with the support of her mother, Ethan slipped off the right side of the mare, came around and gathered the girl in his arms and gave her a great big hug.

"You did fantastic."

She nodded. "Can I do it again?"

He smiled. "You bet."

He was about to let her go when he realized she was too wrung out to use her walker, so he picked her up and carried her to the van. Her mother ran ahead, opened the passenger door, then took over. Almost immediately Daphne closed her eyes and fell asleep.

"Is she all right?" Ethan asked.

"It's been a little overwhelming for her," Shawna said, "but she'll be fine after she rests. Thank you so much for doing this." She shook his hand vigorously. "Can she really come back again?"

"I wouldn't lie to her," he said. "I do need to evaluate the other children who want lessons, though, so it may be a couple of weeks before we can set up a schedule."

"I understand. If there's anything I can do to help… Oh, let me pay you—"

"No charge. The smile on her face is all the pay I want."

A tear coursed down Shawna's cheek. "Thank you, Mr. Ritter."

"Call me Ethan, and you're very welcome. Take good care of her, now."

"I'll call you as soon as we have a schedule worked out," Kayla added.

Shawna kissed her on the cheek. "We'll be waiting."

EVEN WITH ALL the planting done, the vineyard continued to absorb all of Kayla's time and attention until Megan got home from school. She looked out proudly at the rows of young grapevines, regularly checked the newly installed irrigation system and carefully monitored weed and ground cover control. The next three years would tell whether her investment had been worth it, whether it would succeed or fail.

On Wednesday she and Ethan dealt with a ten-year-old boy who had a serious case of Attention Deficit Hyperactivity Disorder.

"Why is he on the list?" Kayla asked. "ADHD

doesn't seem like it's in the same class with the other disabilities we'll be dealing with."

"It's not a physical handicap," Ethan acknowledged, "but it is a disorder that has the potential to benefit from horseback riding. I read up on it over the weekend. Kids—and some adults—with ADHD suffer from very short attention spans. With riding, feedback is immediate. Give a horse the wrong signal and the response is instantaneous—the horse does the wrong thing. No waiting for results, so the person has to concentrate to succeed."

"I hadn't thought of that," Kayla admitted. "Makes sense, though."

She was amazed at the patience Ethan showed with the boy. The session lasted close to half an hour and while Ethan was firm he still managed to convey a sense of teamwork: we're in this together. When the impetuous kid left, both he and his father were smiling. A good sign.

Friday brought Beth Meeks, a nine-year-old blind girl. Worried about her sense of balance, Ethan rode with her for a few minutes to evaluate her equilibrium. When he was satisfied she could handle herself, he let her ride alone, always at a walk, and was pleased when she was able to maintain a reasonably round circle.

During both sessions Megan, Heather and Brad were on the sidelines. To Kayla's relief, her daughter ceased her chattering and observed, calling out encouraging comments only after the rides were over. Heather and Brad were equally respectful, perhaps because they, too, could associate with limitations.

Kayla wondered what Heather's parents had been like. Clearly decent people, for the girl was well mannered and obedient and, while she didn't show it very often, she could also be positive and fun-loving. Had she received any counseling after the accident? Kayla called Leona Rayborn over the weekend and asked.

"Probably," the foster mother replied. "All kids brought into the system undergo a mental evaluation."

"That's not the same as counseling," Kayla remarked, and tried to remember that it wasn't this woman's fault. As aloof as Leona seemed to be sometimes, living with her was probably better than being in an even more impersonal orphanage. "Does she ever talk about her parents?"

"Not to me," Leona said, "and I'm sure not to Randy. Real quiet, that one. Does what she's told. Doesn't give me any trouble. They're not all like that, I can tell you. 'Course, I don't keep them if they give me a hard time. Got enough to do."

"Thanks." Kayla hung up and stared into space. Had no one helped the girl grieve?

That evening she asked Megan if Heather ever talked about her parents.

"I asked her once what they were like," Megan answered. "But she said she didn't want to talk about them. I was afraid she was going to cry."

Brad was also beginning to be protective of her. Megan had recounted two incidents at school where he'd gotten into trouble for pushing boys who were taunting her for being so quiet. He certainly didn't let his handicap inhibit him.

And what about Brad? He was more outspoken and self-assertive than Heather, but Kayla sensed he was holding a lot inside, too. Chances were the boy hadn't received any more professional help to cope with his situation than Heather had. If anything, he probably earned disciplinary action for any rebelliousness. Kayla was willing to spend time with the boy, too, but she wondered if a man couldn't help him more. She'd talk to Ethan about it.

Was she overstepping her bounds? She had no right to ask Ethan to play big brother or surrogate father. He was already doing more than his share by giving the boy free riding lessons.

Yet she was sure he felt the same way she did. She couldn't remember meeting a man, including her father, who was more attuned to kids than Ethan. Some adults condescended to them. A few were overly protective, still others so undemanding and freewheeling that they denied kids the structure they not only needed but craved.

Ethan treated children with the respect they deserved while giving them clear, firm guidance. A woman could love a guy like that.

After Beth left, the children helped Carter bring the horses in from the pasture, and Kayla joined Ethan as he walked Ginger back to the barn.

"It went well today."

"It's been a good week," he agreed. "We'll have to see how the next three sessions go. Different challenges.

"You're good with them," he said in his quiet way. She closed the gate after Ethan released the horse and turned around to find him practically standing on top of her.

Suddenly he had his arms around her and was kissing her. She lost herself in the tantalizing sensation of his mouth on hers.

Then, aware of what she was doing, she pushed him away. "Ethan..." She was breathless. Her heart was pounding. His chest was warm and firm under her palms. "We shouldn't..."

He backed off, but his eyes burned into hers and she knew he wanted to kiss her again.

The shame of knowing she wanted to kiss him, too, despite what Millie had told her, gave vent to anger. "You shouldn't have done that."

At first he just gazed at her, then the meaning of her words seemed to sink in. Hands spread, he backed away. "I'll see you Monday," he mumbled and retreated.

Her pulse was running wild. She couldn't decide who she was more upset with, him or herself.

CARTER WAS ON HIS WAY to the tack room when Ethan stomped through the open barn door and nearly bowled him over.

"Say one word and I'll punch your lights out," Ethan snarled and kept moving.

Carter raised an eyebrow and frowned, then he saw Kayla emerge from the shadows. He scowled as she passed, apparently intent on finding the children. At least that was what he surmised her searching look was supposed to convey.

It would all have been very amusing, if he didn't foresee an unhappy ending. Ethan had sworn off marriage, given up any hope of having children. Even if he were to change his mind about getting hitched, Carter couldn't imagine Kayla being content with a childless union. She was young, healthy and definitely the mothering type.

"Stay out of it, old man," he muttered.

KAYLA PILED THE KIDS into the car and drove down the Broken Spoke's long driveway. Megan and her friends were chattering away about today's new rider.

"She was nicer than that boy who came out last time," Megan commented, making it very clear she didn't think much about boys in general, except maybe Brad.

"It must be hard not being able to see," Heather mused. "I mean, you can't read or watch TV or anything."

"She can read," Brad countered. "Her books have raised letters she feels with her fingers."

"It's called Braille," Kayla explained. "And they're not really letters but little dots."

"I wish I could read Braille," Megan said. "Then I could read in the dark and when we're in the car at night."

Kayla smiled. "The next time you see her, maybe you can ask her to teach you."

"We could all learn," Megan suggested enthusiastically.

The others nodded.

Kayla dropped off the two foster children. She knew they weren't really happy living with the Rayborns, but all her questions, direct and oblique, had resulted in the same answers. They had chores they were supposed to do and they got yelled at if they didn't do them right, but they weren't abused or mistreated, and the food was okay.

A quick stop at the grocery in town for a gallon of milk and a bag of rice to go with tonight's roast chicken, then on home.

The light was beginning to fade as they approached the entrance to the vineyard. Kayla drove around the back of the house and took the dirt road that led over the hill to the vineyard for one last look at the rows of wire and the spindly canes she and her father had planted. Her trained eye automatically scanned the young shoots.

A tinge of brown.

She skidded the car to a stop, throwing Megan against her seat belt.

"Mommy, what's the matter?"

Kayla jumped out of the car and ran to the nearest vine. Rust. No. Something else. She ran to the next row. The same. And the next. She darted between the rows and examined more leaves.

She snatched off small clusters from several vines in different locations, threw them onto the ground at Megan's feet and sped to the house.

She called out to her father, barged into the kitchen and called again. He wasn't there. Megan was trailing behind her. "Mommy, what's wrong?"

Kayla dashed out the door and ran to the old barn, Megan following. "Dad? Where are you?"

Boyd stuck his head out of the workshop, rubbing his hands on an oily rag. "What's up?"

Then he saw his daughter's face. "Kayla? What's the matter?"

"The vines!" she shouted. "Something's happened to them." She offered him the one she was clutching.

He peered at her, then at the tiny buds in her hand.

"They're all like that," she told him.

"This isn't right," he mumbled. "It's not black rot, and it's too early for Pierce's disease. I don't understand…."

"Mommy, what's wrong?" Megan asked again. This time Kayla noticed the child was beginning to wheeze.

"Where's your inhaler, sweetie?" she asked.

"Inside."

"Go back to the house and use it. Then you can do me a big favor by getting the groceries from the car and taking them inside for me. I'll be there in a few minutes to start supper."

"Why are you so mad?" Megan was clearly nervous, her breathing becoming more rapid. "What did I do?"

Kayla crouched in front of her and finger-combed Megan's curly red hair. "You haven't done anything, honey. And I'm not really mad. It's just that I'm worried about our new grape plants."

"Are they sick?"

"I don't know yet. Grandpa and I will have to examine them all very carefully."

"I'm hungry."

Kayla had to smile. "Well, at least I know you're okay. Now go on up to the house and put the groceries away for me, then get busy on your homework. I'll check it while I'm fixing dinner in a little while."

Megan looked skeptical.

"It's okay, sweetheart. I won't be long."

Megan left but not happily.

Boyd had been studying the leaves while his daughter and granddaughter talked.

"Let's see what we have here."

They'd set up a small laboratory in an out-building behind the barn. It wasn't very sophisticated, just a microscope, a few chemicals and test tubes for basic tests, mostly on water and soil samples, but also for identifying bug infestations, fungi and various other common bacterial diseases. If they needed more refined analysis, they sent samples off to a professional lab.

Kayla was searching frantically for an explanation. Her father was right. It was too early for Pierce's disease. Cotton root rot? She'd never run into that particular soil fungus in the Northwest. Her only knowledge of it was from books, but she doubted that was what she was seeing. Besides, it was too early for it to manifest itself. A fungus she hadn't tested the soil for? She was positive she'd covered them all. At least, that's what the county extension service had assured her. A new bacteria? The possibilities seemed endless.

She and her father went around the back of the barn to the tin building where they also stored insecticides, fertilizers and other chemicals. Boyd switched on the lights, and they went directly to the microscope he'd mounted on an old wooden workbench. Positioning a leaf between two thin glass plates, he inserted the slide under the lens. With a frown, he backed away to let her look. She adjusted the focus and peered at the specimen, automatically expecting to find a fungus, tiny mites, larva or some other clue.

Her father removed a reference book from the shelf above her head, flipped through pages of color prints and stared.

Another quick check of the microscope and a comparison with the color slide in the book confirmed his conclusion.

She closed her eyes and took a deep breath. Her heart was pounding.

"Someone's sprayed my vines with herbicide."

CHAPTER SIX

ETHAN AMBLED OVER TO the ringing phone and glanced at the caller ID. Kayla.

His mood instantly brightened, then as quickly sank. Was she calling to tell him he'd stepped over the line when he'd kissed her? He couldn't argue with her. It was true, but she'd also kissed him back, or started to, before she'd decided she wasn't supposed to like it.

"Hello?"

"Ethan, my vineyard's been poisoned." He could hear outrage in her voice.

"Poisoned? How?"

"Someone's sprayed all the plants with herbicide."

"Are you sure?"

"Of course I'm sure," she snapped. "I'll have everything officially tested by a certified lab, but, yes, Dad and I are sure."

"I'll be right over."

When she didn't object, he hung up and ran

out to his truck. Carter was scooping up horse manure from the entrance to the barn.

"Kayla just called. She says someone poisoned her vineyard. I'm going over to see what this is all about."

"Poisoned it?" Carter shook his head. "That's crazy. Who'd do a thing like that?"

"Tell Luella I won't be here for supper, and she shouldn't bother to keep anything for me. I can fix myself a sandwich when I get in."

Carter snorted and shook his head as Ethan drove off.

He pulled up behind Kayla's car a few minutes later. She hadn't expanded the minimal landscaping around the old house, but she had filled the narrow flower beds with colorful pansies and petunias. The shrubs were neatly trimmed.

She was standing in the shade of the porch when he got out of his truck. He remembered what it felt like to hold her and cursed himself. The worried expression on her face made him want to hug her again, but of course that was the last thing he should do now...or ever.

"Come with me." She came down the porch steps and led him to the building the previous owner had used as a storeroom. Inside it was neat and orderly, which didn't surprise him.

At the far end was a workbench with a microscope and several other gadgets, among which he recognized a small centrifuge. He'd never thought about all this paraphernalia being necessary for a vintner or that the cultivation of wine grapes was part art and part science. More or less equal measures of botany, chemistry and intuition.

"I pulled some of the leaves when I saw they were damaged," she explained as she led him to the table. "Take a look."

He hadn't peered into a microscope since high school. This model was much newer and more advanced.

She turned on the back lighting. Adjusting the eyepieces, he stared down at the veins and ridges of a young grape leaf, completely at a loss as to what he was supposed to see or conclude. What he saw appeared to be foreign matter, tiny particles that didn't match their surroundings.

"What am I looking at?" he asked, still bent over.

"The leaf of a vinifera grape. The blackish-brown pinpoints are the cells of a herbicide. Look here."

He raised his head and saw she was pointing

to the page of a textbook. The picture matched what he'd viewed under the magnifying glass.

"Someone has sprayed the entire crop," she said.

His mind tried to consider options, explanations. "Could you or your father have sprayed them with the wrong chemical by mistake?"

She tilted her head. "No, we couldn't," she answered, her indignation sharp as a knife. "I'm not that stupid and neither is my father. We're not opposed to the judicious use of herbicides for weed control, but all our supplies are intact. Besides, it would take a lot more than we keep on hand to spray ten acres. So if you think—"

He held up his hands. "Calm down, Kayla. I'm not accusing you of anything. I'm just asking the kinds of questions the sheriff will ask when you report this."

She sighed in exasperation. "Sorry. You're right."

"When do you suppose this was done?"

Her eyes roamed blindly. "Dad figures, based on the condition of the leaves, probably two or three days ago."

"Where is he, by the way?"

"Making phone calls, arranging for tests—"

"At this hour?" He checked his watch. It was after seven.

"To the West Coast. They're two hours behind us."

He'd forgotten about that. "You were here all day Sunday and yesterday?"

She nodded.

"That leaves Monday when you were over at my place to help with the riding lessons. But your dad was here the whole time, right?"

She shook her head. "He was in town most of the day getting work done on the tractor."

Could that have been sabotaged, too? Ethan tucked that question away for the time being.

"How long would it have taken to do this?" he asked.

She leaned against the bench. "If the person was organized and knew what he was doing, I'd say less than two hours."

"And you were over at my place for at least three."

She agreed.

"Who knew you'd be over there?"

"Probably half the county. It's no secret I go over there to work with you and the kids. Millicent Niebauer has made it public knowledge that we're giving riding lessons."

"Dear Millie. But we really can't blame her. She's just—"

"Doing her job," Kayla finished for him. "Sometimes she does it too well."

He wanted to hold her, to protect her, to reassure her. But how? Her vineyard, her dream and all the work she'd put into it had been ruined.

"It could have been done during the middle of the night, too," Ethan suggested. "We had a full moon the night before last. The weather was so clear you could have read a newspaper by moonlight."

"But why would anyone do this?"

He shook his head, unable to answer her question.

"Do you have an outside light here?" Ethan asked as Kayla started to lock up the workshop.

"Yes," she said, not sure why he was asking.

"Leave it on tonight."

"You think someone will come…? Why? There's nothing here to take."

"But someone could drop something off."

"Like wha— Oh." She finally understood. "You mean like putting empty Roundup containers on my shelves."

"You said yourself you don't normally keep enough around here for a job this size. Whoever's responsible for this has to assume you'll call the sheriff. Seeing a bunch of empty plastic bottles would certainly cast doubt on your story."

"But why would I do this to myself?"

"Insurance?"

She shook her head. "I wouldn't make anything on a claim, even if I could submit one, and I can't do that until I have a crop. Besides, why wouldn't he have left the bottles when he used them?"

Ethan shrugged. "Maybe he didn't want you to find them before the vines were affected for fear you might wash it off."

"It wouldn't have done any good."

"He may not have known that."

"A lot of maybes." She switched on the light over the door and locked the sturdy dead bolt above the knob.

"Mommy, I'm hungry," Megan announced the moment they stepped into the kitchen where she was doing her homework.

"Okay, honey. I'll start dinner now. Ethan is going to eat with us."

"Oh, goodie. Can we have macaroni and cheese?"

"Rice tonight."

Megan made a face.

Boyd appeared in the doorway from the living room. "There was no reason to call you." He went to the refrigerator, got out two cans of Coke and handed one to Ethan. "There's nothing you can do."

"Lend moral support?" Ethan pulled the tab and sucked down the foam that spurted out.

"We can certainly use some of that." Boyd turned to Kayla who was measuring out rice. "I talked to Arnie at the lab in Portland. He wants us to FedEx him a dozen sprigs from different areas."

While the rice cooked, Kayla removed the chicken she'd been marinating from the fridge, and Megan set the table for four. Boyd leaned against the counter near the sink and looked on, preoccupied. Ethan volunteered to grill the chicken on the small backyard patio. Just like a regular family, he thought as he stepped outside and lit the gas grill.

When they sat in the kitchen to eat, he was again struck by the homey atmosphere. Even the smell of the packaged broccoli and cheese, Angela's favorite, conspired against him.

After the four of them had helped clear the table and load the dishwasher, Boyd excused himself to research online before going to bed. While Kayla helped Megan with her bath and put her to bed, Ethan went to the living room and paged through magazines that were mostly about grapes, fruit and nut orchards, truck farming and light agriculture. He was immersed in an article about crop placement and rotation when Kayla finally reemerged from the back of the house.

Her slouched shoulders were the only giveaway that she was tired. "I'm sorry that took so long. She wanted two stories before turning out the light."

"She's a good kid. You and your dad can be real proud of the job you're doing."

"Dad's been a rock, but he only came with us to help get the vineyard started. He plans to go back to Oregon this summer."

"So it'll be just you and Megan. Can't be easy being a single mom."

She shrugged. "Easier, actually, than when Daryl and I were married."

This was the first time she'd ever mentioned her ex-husband.

"What happened—if you don't mind my asking?"

"You don't want to hear my problems."

"Actually I do." He wanted to know everything about this woman.

She gazed at him for an extended moment, then dropped into the easy chair across from him.

"When Megan was first diagnosed with asthma, Daryl glommed on to the doctor's comment that kids often outgrew it. And when that didn't happen soon enough, he insisted it was all psychosomatic, to get attention. It really complicated things, because he seemed to think discipline would solve the problem. He was half-right."

Ethan raised an eyebrow.

"It's not psychosomatic the way he meant it, but emotion definitely contributes to episodes. You saw what happened when she got upset about not taking Birdsong home. Daryl didn't get it that his constant harping and fighting was the biggest cause of her asthma."

"So you divorced him."

She looked sharply at Ethan. "You make it sound like I was the culprit."

"That's not what I meant. I was just stating a fact."

"I divorced him after he walked out," she declared. "And because it was the best way I could protect my daughter."

"I'm sorry."

"I'm not."

"Does she miss him?"

"She misses the idea of him, of having a daddy, but please don't ever ask her about him or bring up his name. It can upset her for days."

The silence between them lingered. "What are you fixin' to do about the vineyard?" he finally asked.

"Replant."

He liked the quick response and the determination he heard in it. "Losing a whole year's growth can't be easy."

"I won't lose a year," she said. "The ideal time for planting new stock is the fall. I missed that when we got here in January, but grapes can actually be planted anytime. I'll tear out what's there now and replant. I won't have lost any significant time, since I wasn't going to get a crop this year, anyway."

"But it'll still cost you."

"The price of new vines," she confirmed. "Not nearly as much as it did when I had to clear the land, install the grid and the irrigation system. I'd move it now, if I could afford to, to a location closer to the house, where I could keep an eye on things better, but I picked that spot because it was the best one."

"How about installing a security system?"

"Too expensive. I don't have that kind of cash

and my savings will be drained when I purchase new stock."

A plan was forming in Ethan's head, but he decided not to say anything about it until he'd had a chance to think it through.

"Who would want to do this, Ethan?" she asked. "What threat could a vineyard possibly be to anyone?"

"A couple of decades back I might have blamed prohibitionists," he said. "Most of Texas didn't go wet until the mid-eighties, and there are a few counties that're still dry. Not that that's an issue anymore. Never was in Loveless County. Although you still have to go outside city limits for hard liquor. But your vineyard isn't designed exclusively for the local market anyway."

"So why? I don't understand."

"There was a lot of controversy when Miranda proposed the Home Free concept. Our consortium, KC Enterprises, had just gone bust and everyone was wondering what was going to happen. Everyone expected Clint Gallagher—" He paused. "Everyone figured he'd buy it, since it touched his spread and would have made him the biggest rancher in several counties around."

"This consortium," she said, "the Broken Spoke was part of it, wasn't it?"

Ethan nodded. "My father was one of its organizers, along with Nate Cantrell, Jock Montgomery—"

"The sheriff?"

"His father. Robert Bell, Jase Farley and Nan Wright, the mayor's mother. Some put in cash, a lot of it, for a few of them it was their life savings. Others, like Jase and my father, who were cash poor, contributed their land to the venture."

"So when it failed, everybody lost. Was your father blamed?"

"He blamed himself. Felt he should have seen what was coming."

"In what way?"

"KC Enterprises had borrowed a lot of money from the bank to increase stock, drill new water wells, install fencing. Then the drought hit, and the bank refused to extend us any more credit. We could have weathered even that crisis by selling off cattle, if the mad cow disease scare hadn't struck. Foreign markets shut down and beef prices fell so low it didn't even pay to haul the stock to market."

"I heard Gallagher blocked the loan," Kayla said, "so he could buy up the place."

Ethan nodded. "Would have worked, too, if

Miranda hadn't come up with her harebrained scheme."

"If everybody thought Miranda's idea was so crazy, how did it get implemented?"

Ethan laughed. "You don't know Miranda. Once she latches on to something, she doesn't give up. Arlen Enfield was our mayor then, and chummy with Gallagher, if not exactly in his pocket. He refused to put the matter on the city council agenda, so she ran against him in the next election. People laughed at first. Enfield had been in office for twelve years, and his re-election was considered a slam dunk, but she made Home Free the focus of her campaign. When she won, I don't think anyone was more surprised than Enfield, or maybe Gallagher. Anyway, her first order of business was Home Free. It passed the council by a narrow margin."

"Do you think Enfield could be behind this?"

"I can't imagine why. What would he have to gain at this point? He's out of office. Wrecking the Home Free program won't put him back in. Besides, I think he's already looking at other options, like replacing Gallagher in the state senate."

Ethan shook his head. "If I had to point in any one direction, I'd be more inclined to pick Gallagher himself. Most of the land still hasn't been given away, but no one's allowed to buy more than one parcel, which means he can't just walk in and buy them all up. I imagine that sticks in his craw. On the other hand, if he were to scare enough people off, and the project failed, he'd be in an excellent position to make an offer for it."

"But he's a state senator," she objected, "and he already has a big ranch. What would he need more land for?"

"Pride, a sense of entitlement, prestige. Trust me, Clint Gallagher didn't become a power broker in Austin by being a nice guy. He's a cutthroat politician of the old school." Ethan shrugged. "Of course this is all speculation."

He rose from the couch. "It's late and I'm sure you have things to do. Call the sheriff in the morning and let me know what time he's coming out. I'll be over to meet him with you."

CHAPTER SEVEN

KAYLA STOOD ON the front porch and watched him drive off. She'd half expected him to kiss her good-night. In fact, she'd been tempted to give him a peck on the cheek, like when he'd given her the neck and shoulder massage. She could still see the surprise on his face and remember the kiss in the barn. Dangerous territory, but then, she'd known he was dangerous from the first moment she saw him.

Life was becoming too complicated. She didn't need to make matters worse by giving in to the attraction she felt for Ethan. Not when he was so close; when she felt so needy and so vulnerable.

After fixing herself a cup of tea she sat at the kitchen table, wishing he was still sitting across from her. She forced herself to review the hazards of late planting.

Other than adjusting the watering schedule and spreading net over the new canes to protect them from scorching, there seemed few downsides. The vines would still have the long growing season to establish themselves before autumn pruning.

Worry about her vineyard made Kayla restless that night, but that was only part of the problem. It had been a long time since she'd had a man of her own generation to talk to, to lean on, to share concerns with, and now the one person she'd found just happened to be a smart, caring, fun-loving, very attractive eligible bachelor.

She rolled out of bed on schedule in the morning, showered quickly, dressed and went to the kitchen. Her father was already up, sipping coffee and looking over a list of things to do that day.

"What time are you calling the sheriff?" he asked after greeting her.

"I'll wait until I get Megan off to school. I also want to check the workshop and vineyard one more time."

He gazed at her, eyebrows raised.

She laughed when she realized she hadn't answered his question. "Probably around eight."

"I heard about a small used John Deere coming into the Weed and Feed today. I thought I'd check it out, since our tractor seems to be beyond economic redemption. A cultivator comes with it, which we could also use. If they're any good, they'll sell fast, so I ought to get there early."

"Go ahead. I can deal with the sheriff."

"You told me Ritter offered to come over. I think you ought to take him up on it. He's from here. He might be able to help the sheriff figure out what's going on."

Kayla almost smiled. Was her father playing matchmaker? Wouldn't be the first time since her divorce.

If the attack on her vineyard was part of a larger plan to destroy the Home Free program, she wasn't the only one in danger. Other new landowners, Ethan included, were at risk. She didn't want to be responsible if something happened to his horses or if someone on another parcel of land got hurt.

"I will," she promised. "But let me get you and Megan on your way first."

She'd prepared Irish oatmeal, which he liked and Megan tolerated, and soon saw them both out the door. She had no doubt her father would stop off at the café in town and indulge in a "proper" breakfast of sausage and eggs, skillet-fried potatoes and biscuits dripping with butter. She smiled fondly. Every time his cholesterol was checked, it was on the low side. Go figure.

Precisely at eight she telephoned the sheriff's office.

She'd met Wade Montgomery briefly when she'd first come to town and again at Zeb's burial. He seemed like a pleasant enough guy. The question was how competent was he?

"Hello, Mrs. Price," he said when the receptionist put her through. "What can I do for you?"

She explained what she'd found the evening before.

"I'll be out in about an hour." He hung up. He hadn't asked for any details. Was that a good sign?

She phoned Ethan. He picked up on the first ring.

"I'm on my way." No hesitation.

She got another mug from the cabinet and set it on the table. Ethan tapped on her back door ten minutes later. She realized, as she opened it, that it would have felt perfectly natural for him to simply walk in. As dangerous as he was to her equilibrium, she didn't feel threatened by him.

"Black, right?" she asked as she filled his cup.

"Yeah, thanks." He removed his down vest and hung it on the back of a chair before sitting. "You said you couldn't afford to move the vineyard, that you'll have to replant in the same place."

She took the seat across from him. Why did his shoulders seem so wide this morning? "Right. Too expensive to prepare new ground. It's also the best location, one I can expand easily."

He sipped his coffee. "Since you can't see it from the house, the only way you're going to keep it under surveillance is with security cameras."

She shook her head. "I told you yesterday I can't afford that kind of high-tech equipment."

"You can't afford not to have it, Kayla. If whoever's responsible for this comes back a second time, you'll be out of business."

"And out of here," she added. "Which apparently is what he wants."

"We keep saying 'he,'" Ethan pointed out, "but this could just as easily have been done by a woman."

Kayla raised a brow. "You're right, of course."

They drank their coffee in silence.

"The town is offering low-interest loans to new buyers," he said a minute later. "You qualify."

"They're only for building or renovating

houses, clearing land, planting crops. I've already explained that I don't want to relocate—" The light came on. "Oh, you mean if I take out a loan for my new vines, I can use my own cash reserves to install a security system."

"One that's monitored 24/7 by professionals. That way you won't have to worry about trespassers in the middle of the night or when you can't be home."

"It's a good idea," she agreed, "but expensive."

"Not nearly as expensive as having someone pull this stunt again. I have another suggestion."

"What's that?"

"List me as an alternate contact if your surveillance service detects trespassers and can't get hold of you or if you're too far away to respond."

"I couldn't ask you to assume that kind of responsibility."

"It's no big deal. I imagine the service would want to check with you before reporting violators to verify that the apparent trespassers don't have a legitimate right to be on the property. Put me and Carter down as alternate contacts. If none of us can be reached within a specified period of time, say three minutes, or we don't know who the stranger is, they'll notify the sheriff's office."

She rotated her cup. He was becoming a part of her life, her support system. As agreeable as the idea was, it also frightened her. She didn't like being dependent. Leaning on her father was one thing… "That's very generous, but—"

"This is what neighbors here do, Kayla." He looked her straight in the eye, and she realized this wasn't about them. At least, not exclusively. "We look out for each other. It's really no burden. If a trespasser comes on your place, I can react a lot faster than the sheriff. I also have a vested interest. A threat against you puts me and mine at risk. I have high-dollar horses on my place. I can't afford to have them poisoned or injured. Once word of this incident gets out—and it will, thanks to Millicent—I could be ruined. Without confidence that the horses people entrust to me are safe, owners won't bring them and I'll be out of business."

The doorbell rang. Kayla gazed at Ethan for a few seconds, then went to answer it, aware of him following her.

"Mrs. Price." The sheriff tipped his Stetson as he stood on her step.

"Please call me Kayla. Come in. You know Ethan."

The two men shook hands.

"Would you like coffee, Sheriff?"

"Better not. Why don't you show me the vineyard?"

The three went out to the scene of the crime. She showed him the damaged leaves.

"You sure this was done with herbicide? It's not a problem in the soil?"

She led him to the workshop, showed him what she'd showed Ethan the night before.

"I'll take fresh samples of leaves and stems from various parts of the vineyard now. I'd like you to sign across the seals on the envelopes I put them in. You can also sign your name on the FedEx container, then I'll get them off to a reputable laboratory in Oregon for analysis."

"Thorough. Good chain of evidence," he said. "I like that. Any idea who might have done this?"

She shook her head. "Everyone here has been so friendly and supportive. I haven't had a hint that I've been making enemies."

"Have you found the source of the herbicide? The bottles or containers it came in, whatever was used as an applicator?"

"No. Dad and I checked every row but haven't found anything that looks even remotely suspicious. Except that all my vines are dying," she added.

"How about you?" Wade asked Ethan, who'd been tagging along without saying a word, letting Kayla handle it herself.

"I personally walked our common fence line at first light and came up equally dry. No sign of any trespassers, but I'm on the west, between here and the Four Aces. Whoever did this probably came in from the south, from the properties that haven't sold yet. It's all still open range. The only thing separating it from Kayla's property is a four-foot wire fence—not much of an obstacle."

The sheriff nodded. "Easy access. Ever seen anyone?"

"I go riding out there sometimes and occasionally see kids on off-road vehicles. It wouldn't be difficult for someone to drive close to her fence, crawl over or under it, poison her vineyard and be gone without being detected."

"ATVs are pretty loud."

"Not if they stayed in one of the gullies. A bit more of a problem at night, when things are quiet, but if everybody is sleeping and the windows are closed—"

"We have to keep our windows closed and

the air-circulating system going," Kayla explained, "because of Megan's asthma."

"So you probably wouldn't hear anybody in the middle of the night."

She shook her head. "Not unless they're exceptionally noisy."

"What about during the day? Is someone always here?"

"Most of the time, but not always. Dad has been spending time in town trying to get our tractor fixed. In fact he's there now looking at a replacement. And I'm gone for several hours Monday, Wednesday and Friday afternoons, when I take Megan and a couple of her classmates over to the Broken Spoke for riding lessons."

Wade added the information to the notes he'd been scribbling in a small pad. "What are your plans now?" he asked.

She made brief eye contact with Ethan. "Install a security system with sensors and cameras."

"Expensive," Wade noted.

"Apparently the cost of doing business here in paradise is sky-high," she said with an ironic grin. "Now I have a question for you, Sheriff. What are you going to do about this?"

He closed his notebook and put it in his

breast pocket. "I'll check out the surrounding land, see if I can find anything, file a report, of course, and start asking questions."

He rose from his seat. "But I have to be honest with you, Kayla. Without some kind of hard evidence that'll tie someone else to what's happened, there isn't much I can do. It could have been kids having fun or someone out to ruin you, but for all I know, you poisoned those plants yourself. The fact is, I have no proof a crime's been committed."

Her mouth dropped open. "Why would I poison my own vineyard?"

"I'm not saying you did or that you did it intentionally," the lawman clarified. "It could have been by accident."

She felt her blood pressure rise. "You think I'd move here from a thousand miles away, spend tens of thousands of dollars to plant a vineyard, buy select cuttings, devote hundreds of hours in backbreaking work planting them, then be so incompetent that I'd spray with Roundup and kill them all? Having ruined myself, I'd call the law and try to blame it on someone else? Thanks a lot, Sheriff. I can see I'm not going to get much help from you. Sorry I wasted your time—and mine. You might as well leave right now."

"I didn't say—"

"Just go, Sheriff."

He looked at Ethan, as if expecting the man to bail him out. All Ethan did was open the workshop door for him.

"I don't believe it," Kayla fumed after the sheriff's car had pulled out of the driveway.

"Wade's a good guy," Ethan insisted. "He overplayed the devil's advocate role just now, but he's on your side."

"I hate to think what he'd be like if he wasn't," she snapped.

Before she realized it was happening, he had his arms around her, rubbing her back. She needed to keep her distance from this man. Instead, she found herself pressing her cheek against the soft flannel of his shirt, far too aware of the hard chest beneath it. She hadn't intended to seek physical comfort from him, but she couldn't resist it when it was offered.

She started to step back, but he kept her trapped in his embrace. An instant later his lips were on hers.

She tried to remind herself she didn't want to kiss him.

When they broke off a minute later, she still clung to him.

"We'll get through this," he murmured.

We? she wondered when they finally separated.

LATER THAT MORNING, Kayla dropped off the package of damaged leaves at FedEx for overnight delivery to the laboratory in Portland. From there she visited city hall to apply for a low-interest loan to replace her stock. She was filling out the paperwork when Miranda Wright came into the county clerk's office.

"Oh, Kayla, hi. I heard what happened out at your place. It's absolutely terrible. I'm so sorry. It must be heartbreaking to put in all that work and have it ruined."

So the sheriff had informed the mayor. Had he also expressed suspicion that she herself had poisoned the vineyard? "Who would do a thing like that?"

Miranda shook her head. "I'm as baffled by it as you are. Sheriff Montgomery seems to think it might have been kids."

Kayla wondered if he really believed that, or if he was just trying to downplay the situation. Ethan said he was an honest lawman, but could he have some other reason for casting doubt on the incident?

"I don't think so," Kayla said. At Miranda's

quizzical expression, she explained, "It was done too methodically. Only the grapes were touched. I'd expect kids to be more indiscriminate, less organized and neat. There wasn't any debris, not even the containers the herbicide came in."

Miranda pursed her lips. "I see your point, but I really can't imagine who else would do a thing like that."

"None of your other new home owners have had problems like this?"

"Why should they?" Miranda asked.

Kayla didn't miss the defensiveness in her response or that she didn't answer the question.

"Just wondering." Kayla had the feeling Miranda wasn't being completely candid. "The sheriff better figure it out soon," she warned. "They got me. They can get other people. By the way, Millicent at the *Herald* called me this morning. She wants an interview. I'll probably stop by and give her one later today. I figure the more people who know about this the more alert they'll be, and maybe someone will remember hearing or seeing something and come forward."

"Oh, well, yes, I suppose that's true." But she didn't say it with conviction. Kayla understood why the mayor wasn't eager to have word of this incident getting out. The *Herald* didn't have a very large circulation, but that didn't mean the story wouldn't get picked up by one of the bigger media outlets in San Antonio, Austin, Dallas or Houston. Negative publicity could put a damper on the Home Free program.

After receiving Miranda's assurance that her loan application wouldn't be a problem, Kayla stopped by Wade Montgomery's office in the back of the courthouse. A decent guy who'd overplayed his hand, Ethan had said. She'd probably overreacted, too. It didn't seem like a good idea to alienate the sheriff of the county she lived in.

He rose from his chair when she was shown in, then invited her to sit.

"I'm afraid you misunderstood me this morning," he said after resuming his own chair, his hands folded on the desk. "I wasn't accusing you of anything, merely laying out the case as it might look to an outsider."

She supposed that was as close to an apology as she was likely going to get. "That's what Ethan said after you left." She didn't remind him that Ethan had held the door for him. "I apologize for jumping to the wrong conclusion."

He visibly relaxed. "I didn't handle it well,

but now that you're here, let me fill you in on the progress of my investigation so far."

So he was taking the matter seriously. At least that was encouraging.

"I've checked with our local ranch and garden supply stores to see if anyone has purchased large quantities of Roundup or any other nonselective herbicides in the past ninety days. Maude Higgins bought a quart a few weeks ago, but she hasn't used it yet. Max Forster bought a quart, too, but that was yesterday. It's still sitting on his garage shelf. Knowing Max, it'll probably still be there this time next year."

"How about sprayers?" Kayla asked.

"They're a special-order item, and there haven't been any requests in over a year."

"So it wasn't bought around here."

"I'm checking gardening shops in San Antonio, but with all the landscapers there…" He shrugged. "Anything less than a pallet probably wouldn't be treated as an exceptional sale, a lot more than I understand it would take to cover ten acres."

He was right. She stood. "Well, thanks for trying."

"I haven't given up, Ms. Price. I still have a few avenues to pursue."

"Kayla," she reminded him. "And they're all

long shots. I understand that. I appreciate your efforts nevertheless, Sheriff."

He, too, had gotten up and was coming around the desk. "I am sorry about this morning." He extended his hand.

She took it.

"I'll keep you posted."

"Thanks again." She was almost at the door when she remembered the second reason she'd come to see him. "Can you recommend a good security service?"

He seemed pleased that she would seek his advice. "Diep Protection handles surveillance for the Four Aces. I've gotten calls from them a few times. Always been very professional, though the incidents all turned out to be false alarms. There's another outfit—" he went to his desk and took out a bunch of business cards from his middle drawer "—Delucca Security. They're new in this area. I haven't worked with them, but they have a good reputation." He handed her the card.

"Thanks. I'll check them out and let you know what I decide."

The air seemed clearer, the day a bit brighter, when she stepped out of the sheriff's office. Except that burying the hatchet with Montgomery didn't change the fact that her vineyard had been wiped out.

It was lunchtime, so she stopped by Bertha's Kolaches across from the courthouse for a sandwich.

The owner, Bertha Golchak, had been running the old-fashioned lunchroom since the Battle of the Bulge—literally. A yellowed newspaper article over the cash register showed her standing beside the entrance more than sixty years before. Her specialty, then as now, was kolaches, small Czech pastries filled with various fruits or nuts.

At ninety, Bertha admitted she was beginning to slow down. She didn't do much of the cooking herself anymore, though she still served and collected the money at a cash register that had a crank on the side. She hadn't rung anything up on the antique in years. "Real good cigar box," she often claimed.

"Yep." The elderly woman poured coffee into a thick ceramic mug. "Your daddy was in here earlier. Had creamed beef on toast and one of my apricot kolaches."

Kayla shook her head, smiling. But she grew serious when the woman behind the counter offered condolences about her ruined vineyard.

Kayla ate a chicken salad on wheat toast and

was about to ask for the check when the wizened old woman waved a raspberry-walnut kolache under her nose. "Last one," Bertha crooned with a fiendish grin, showing her store-bought teeth.

Ah, sweet temptation.

From there, Kayla went to the library where she ran internet checks on the two security companies Wade had suggested. Since Ethan believed so strongly that Senator Gallagher was involved in this mess, she gave Diep Protection only a cursory glance.

Ethan had mentioned Delucca as well, which tended to tip the scales for her, but she queried both nevertheless, telling them concisely what she wanted. She left her home e-mail address.

Her last stop before driving home was the *Herald* office. Millicent was waiting for her, pen and pad ready at hand.

She conducted a very professional interview. Then came the inevitable silly questions reporters seemed obsessed with these days: How did it make you feel?

Well, I was caught between this urge to skip rope and chew gum at the same time, but settled on just getting really ticked off instead.

"Very discouraged," she said, "then I got mad. My father and I put a lot of work into that vineyard. I'm not about to let someone destroy it, not without a fight."

"What are you fixing to do?" Millicent asked.

"Replant. This time, though, I'll have top-notch security in place. If anyone trespasses on my property again, I'll know it, and I'll be able to identify him...or her. I can also promise you that I'll file criminal charges. Fool me once, shame on me. Mess with me twice and you're toast."

Millie's expression was filled with admiration. "You have another story to tell, too, Kayla, don't you? A much happier one. Tell me about this therapeutic riding program you and Ethan Ritter have started."

Kayla's passion took over. Without using names or specifying handicaps that would identify their clients, she told Millie about the children they'd put on horses for the first time last week.

"Will you be establishing a permanent program?"

"We're still evaluating that," Kayla said. "There's an organization, PATH International, the Professional Association of Therapeutic Horsemanship, which trains and certifies instructors for disabled children and adults.

We're looking into joining. A lot will depend on how much interest there is and whether we can persuade volunteers to help us. As you can imagine, there's more to it than just putting people on horses and letting them ride around by themselves. They need close supervision and hands-on support."

"And it really helps these children?"

Kayla smiled. "It's impossible to ride a horse and not use your muscles. Physical therapy is inherent even when the rider isn't aware of being part of it. What we're doing is rudimentary right now, but it's a beginning."

"How can people contact you if they're interested in participating or helping out?"

Kayla hadn't been prepared for this question, though it was a logical one. She certainly couldn't put the burden on Ethan. Picking up her cell phone, she made a call, then told Millicent, "They can call Noah Kelley at his home." She gave his telephone number.

Millie closed her pad. "What you and Ethan are doing is wonderful. Of course, given what happened to his sister, I suppose we should all have expected it of him."

"I saw her tombstone out at the ranch," Kayla admitted. "She was so young."

"Fourteen. Such a sweet girl, too."

"What happened? I've been reluctant to ask Ethan."

"It's a sad story," Millicent said and refilled both their coffee cups.

CHAPTER EIGHT

"ANGELA ATE CANDY THAT was made in Mexico. Tamarind candy. Very popular there. What no one knew at the time was that it was contaminated with lead."

"Oh, no!"

"Apparently the vats used in manufacturing it contained high amounts of lead, which leached into the candy. Even the paper it was wrapped in was contaminated. Angela loved the stuff. Ethan occasionally ate it, too, but not nearly as much. Angela had been eating it for over a year when Luella, the housekeeper, discovered it. She'd heard rumors of it being tainted, so she told Valerie. Both children— Angela was eight at the time, Ethan fourteen— had to be tested. Turned out they both came up positive for lead poisoning."

Kayla shuddered at the thought of what their parents must have gone through. Candy. It was unconscionable.

"The kids underwent chelation. You know what that is?"

"A process to wash the blood, isn't it?"

Millicent nodded. "When it was over, the doctors declared Ethan clean, but not Angela. The damage to her liver, kidneys and brain was already done and it was irreversible."

Kayla closed her eyes and bit her lip. "Did they take legal action against the company?" she asked.

Millie screwed up her mouth in disgust. "For all the good it did. Personal injury lawsuits against domestic companies can be difficult enough, but this outfit was in Mexico and since the candy hadn't been exported for sale—or consumed in Mexico—there was a question whether Americans even had a right to sue. Still the Ritters joined a class-action suit against the candy maker, but nothing ever came of it. For one thing, as soon as the suit was filed, the company disbanded and the owners disappeared. Ethan's folks finally had to give up. Even if they'd won, chances are they wouldn't have gotten much after lawyers on both sides of the border had taken their cut, plus legal fees."

Kayla shook her head. "So did insurance cover their expenses?"

"Most of the tests and the chelation, but beyond that there really wasn't much they could do. Over the next six years Angela got worse and worse. She stopped growing. Her physical coordination deteriorated, so did her mind. She still loved horses, though, so Ethan took her riding every day—"

"On Birdsong," Kayla said, almost in a whisper. No wonder he didn't want to sell her.

Millicent nodded.

"Even after Angela was confined to a wheelchair and became too weak to sit in the saddle by herself, he would place her in front of him and hold her while they rode bareback."

Kayla pictured Ethan cradling Daphne Jones against his chest as they circled the arena. What painful memories that must have evoked for him.

"Eventually Angela became bedridden." Millicent's voice was soft and shaky. "By the time she died she was little more than skin and bones, her mind completely gone."

Kayla brushed away a tear.

"Tore the family apart, as you might imagine," Millie added. "Valerie passed away in her sleep a year later. They say it was heart failure, but if you ask me the poor woman died of a broken heart."

If anything ever happened to Megan... Kayla rose from the chair. "Thank you for telling me. It helps me understand why he's so sympathetic, so good with the children."

The older woman accompanied her to the door. "It's too bad the Rayborns will be leaving."

Heather and Brad's foster parents? "Leaving? Where are they going?"

"My sources tell me Chicago," Millicent whispered, though there was no one around. "I reckon being foster parents pays better up there. Bless their hearts."

"What'll happen to the children?"

"They'll get thrown back into the system and shuffled off to other foster parents. All we can hope for is that whoever inherits them are as good to them as Leona and Randy have been."

Good? Ethan's words came back to her. *Why does 'good' not sound good enough?*

Moving Heather and Brad, disrupting their lives again, would be devastating. The Broken Spoke was the one bright spot in their lives. Heather was finally beginning to emerge from her shell, and Brad seemed to be letting go of his anger. Even though they weren't related, they'd begun to bond like brother and sister, too. Taking them away and probably separating them in the process would be traumatic, bordering on abuse.

There must be something she could do about it.

ETHAN HAD BEEN THINKING all morning about what had happened at Kayla's vineyard. Was someone out to ruin Kayla or her father? That didn't make sense. They were new to the area, had hardly been in Texas long enough to have created enemies. The truth was, everybody liked them. At least, that's what Luella reported.

Of course, they could have made enemies in the Northwest who had followed them here, but that didn't seem likely. The only thing that made sense was that it was someone intent on undermining the Home Free program by scaring away newcomers to the area. The question was who, and what would they have to gain?

Clint Gallagher. Ethan had initially been skeptical of his father's insistence that the senator was behind the consortium's collapse. Zeb had been bitter at the time and looking for someone to blame for the failure of the enterprise he'd played such a prominent role in organizing and the loss of the ranch his family had owned for over a hundred and twenty years.

The wily politician was ambitious and seemed to grow more desperate in the past few years. Pursuing a legacy, some claimed. Nearly doubling the size of the Four Aces before he died would certainly qualify. It was no secret he'd expected to pick up the consortium's holdings after it went bust, not just for the prestige, but because it controlled the aquifer that watered Gallagher's land. Water was sacred in Texas. Control of it meant power, and there was no question that Gallagher thrived on power.

Ethan finished his second session of the day with Duke and turned him loose in the corral. The gelding was progressing nicely, but it would be a long time before he trusted people. Still, he'd permitted Ethan to put a saddle pad on him, then a saddle. This time Ethan had even gotten it buckled. Maybe tomorrow he'd be able to get on the horse's back. They wouldn't go anywhere. Ethan would just sit there so Duke would understand he wasn't being threatened. Bragging to Carter that he'd be riding the skittish horse by the end of the week might have been premature, but achieving the goal wasn't too far off.

Ethan couldn't understand people who bought animals, then neglected or mistreated them. But there were many. Sometimes it was out of ignorance—like feeding them too much rich grain, thinking they were giving them a treat. Sometimes it was out of frustration—short-tempered people who couldn't seem to comprehend that an animal's response was immediate and elementary: seek comfort, avoid pain. But there were also those who enjoyed the power trip over weaker creatures, whether they were animals or other human beings.

As he returned tack to its proper place, his mind was already on Kerwin, the handicapped child who was coming out to the Broken Spoke in a couple of hours. Ethan had spoken to the boy's father on the phone last week. According to Jim, his nine-year-old son had been born with deformed upper extremities, a foreshortening of the arms that amounted to having no arms at all. He was also a near genius. Ethan accepted the later evaluation with reserve. Parents were often the worst judges of their children's abilities, oftentimes prone to exaggerating their intelligence to counterbalance other shortcomings, real or imagined. Like the straight-A student who was a complete klutz in sports; the star athlete who couldn't count out change. On the other hand, there were people who compensated amazingly well for one physical handicap with extraordinary capabilities in other areas.

Jim also explained that he and his wife didn't give their son any slack. Within the boy's capabilities, Ethan didn't plan to, either.

Kayla's vehicle tore up the driveway, raising a cockscomb of fine dust behind it. Ethan's spirits instantly rose. She was making him crazy, but being near her was preferable to being away from her. Look but don't touch was becoming increasingly difficult. He'd kissed her twice now, and she'd kissed him back both times. Which only made him want to get closer to her. It would have been better if she'd slapped his face—or would it? He'd always loved a challenge.

The children piled out of the Toyota and shouted a cheerful greeting as they ran toward the barn to get their horses groomed and saddled.

Ethan watched as Kayla slid from behind the wheel and walked toward him. A pretty sight. The sway of her hips, the sun glinting off her auburn hair. She looked intense, preoccupied. Understandable, considering her situation.

The kids' lesson went well. They all seemed to be in sync that afternoon. He had them do interlocking circles at a walk and trot, reverse course and repeat the drill. Megan was still bouncing too much in the saddle and Brad was inclined to go faster than the two girls, but they managed nevertheless to hold it together. He was pleased, and it was easy to see they felt good about their performances, too.

They'd already put their horses out to pasture and started cleaning stalls when a slightly battered pickup rolled up the driveway. A man in his thirties got out the driver's side, a boy, the other.

Kerwin Delgado was tall for a ten-year-old, his eyes startlingly blue against his black hair. The sleeves of his T-shirt had been modified to expose his hands, which appeared to project directly from unexpectedly wide shoulders.

"Jim Delgado." He shook Ethan's hand. "Thanks for inviting us out. This is my son, Kerwin."

"I've always wanted to ride a horse," the boy said in a voice that was still prepubescent, but with a maturity that belied his age.

"Well, this is your lucky day," Ethan told him. "Come on over, and I'll introduce you to Lottie."

The mare was tied to the hitching post just outside the barn. Ethan went through the usual orientation, having the boy let the animal sniff him. Having him pet her neck and rub her eyes.

"How old is she?" Kerwin asked.

"Sixteen."

"Is that old for a horse?"

"What did the internet tell you?" Ethan asked.

Kerwin looked at him and grinned. "That the oldest horse on record was fifty-six, that in captivity they can frequently live into their thirties while in the wild they probably don't survive much past ten."

Ethan smiled. Maybe Jim had been right about his son's IQ.

"We take good care of our animals. When I was about your age we had a mare that lived to be thirty-seven."

"Did she have any teeth left?" the boy asked.

Ethan chuckled. "Not many. By then we were hand-feeding her cooked oatmeal, but old Savannah still seemed to enjoy living, so we didn't mind."

"Who's your oldest horse here now?"

"Birdsong," Megan piped up.

She and the other children were just coming out of the barn, Brad limping behind a wheelbarrow full of manure, the girls carrying rakes. The three stole glances at the newcomer's strange deformity, then seemed to accept it.

"She's my horse," Megan announced. "I love her."

Kerwin continued to rub Lottie's nose. "Can I ride now?"

"Come on." Ethan untied the lead rope and led the mare to the mounting block and moved to the horse's right side. "How's your sense of balance?" he asked.

Kerwin climbed the tall steps, then paused, waiting for direction. "I swim and play soccer."

Swimming would explain the wide shoulders and upper body development.

"Put your left foot in the left stirrup and throw your right leg over the saddle. I'll catch you if you go too far."

"I won't," the boy said confidently.

And he didn't, though he was a bit unsteady at first, when the stirrup shifted as he tucked his boot into it.

"Can you reach down and grab the reins?"

The boy bent forward and grasped them with his left hand, then rotated his shoulders to clasp them with his right as well.

As the session began, Ethan evaluated the boy's control and stability. Clearly he had strong legs, no doubt from playing soccer, and while he lacked a certain amount of manual dexterity, he seemed adaptable and eager to try whatever he was asked.

"Can I trot now?" the boy called out after fifteen minutes of walking in straight lines and circles in both directions.

Ethan hesitated. Kerwin sat the horse well, but trotting usually didn't come until at least the second lesson, and the kids usually grabbed hold of the saddle horn, an option Kerwin obviously didn't have. A glance over at Jim convinced him, however, that it would be all right.

After telling the boy what to do, Ethan gave Lottie the verbal signal to move out. Kerwin bounced uncontrollably.

"Relax," Ethan called out. "Stretch your legs down and lean back."

The boy struggled to comply, then regained control. He wasn't graceful, but he stayed on and kept his back straight, his heels down.

"Neat," the boy said. "What am I doing wrong?"

Ethan couldn't help but grin. "Think of it this way," he said. "The tighter you squeeze a watermelon seed between your fingers, the farther it shoots. Stay limber and go with the flow." On the second attempt the boy did better.

The lesson lasted a full hour, much longer than usual for a first session. But the kid's enthusiasm and eagerness to learn were insatiable and infectious.

While Kerwin cooled the horse, Ethan went over to talk to his father. "I'm impressed," he admitted. "He's got considerable athletic ability."

Jim smiled proudly. "There really isn't much he can't do."

"He's a lucky kid," Ethan said with sincerity, "to have parents who don't coddle him."

"We wouldn't be doing him any favors if we did. He'll never be a concert pianist or a violinist, but then, few of us are."

Ethan laughed. "I'm sure not. He's going to be sore tonight and tomorrow."

Jim chuckled. "Serves him right for showing off. Don't worry. He'll get over it." He grew more serious. "I'll pay whatever you charge for lessons. I don't want him receiving any special treatment."

"Let's set up a schedule," Ethan offered. He'd already decided this kid didn't belong in the therapeutic group. With Kerwin it would be standard riding lessons.

KAYLA LAY AWAKE most of Monday night worrying.

What would become of Heather and Brad if

they were separated? If they could no longer come out to the Broken Spoke?

And the vineyard. Suppose her father couldn't find enough cuttings suitable to this area?

Most of all, what about the feelings developing between her and Ethan? She'd vowed after her divorce not to get involved with anyone. It made things too complicated, not just for her, but for Megan. Life was difficult enough for an eight-year-old with asthma who'd been abandoned by her dad.

After seeing Megan off to school Tuesday, Kayla decided she had no choice.

The Child Protective Services office for Loveless County was located in a small stucco building a block behind the courthouse. The inside was as bleak as the outside, soulless, crowded with file cabinets and untidy stacks of paper. Kayla walked up to the counter.

"May I help you?" the woman at a desk in the far corner asked across the room.

"I'd like to apply to become a foster parent."

The woman didn't seem in the least impressed, much less cheered at the announcement.

"Actually for two particular children," Kayla added. "I understand the people who are taking care of them now will be leaving the area.

I know the children and would like them to come and live with us."

"Are you related to them?"

Kayla shook her head. "They're in the same class as my daughter."

The woman dropped the papers she'd been sorting onto the cluttered desktop and rose. She was a mountain of a woman in a dark blue dress that hung on her like a tent.

"I can't help you," she said. "We'll be closing this office in a few weeks." She waved her hand at the chaos. "I'm sorting through records now, purging before transferring the lot to the San Antonio office."

"Closing? But why?"

"Homestead doesn't meet the population requirements to have its own office."

"But with all the new people moving in to take advantage of the Home Free program—"

"The decision to close was made last year. At that time the town had been in decline for several years."

"But surely now—"

"A few new families have recently located here, but not enough to reverse the decision. Homestead's status will be reevaluated in three years."

"Three years?"

"Officials at the state level can consider opening a satellite office here before then, but I wouldn't count on it. Everybody's consolidating these days. Can't afford to keep a staff in every little town and village. Inefficient."

"What's going to happen to the children who are already in foster care here?"

"You say the family is relocating. Where to, do you know?"

"Chicago, I think."

"Leaving the state. In that case, the children will eventually be sent to other families within Texas."

"Eventually?" Kayla was aghast. "Where will they go in the meantime?"

"There's a group home in San Antonio," the woman responded without any indication the sentence she'd just pronounced bothered her in the least. Maybe it didn't. Maybe she really didn't care. Maybe to her they were simply statistics on a chart.

"There must be something I can do," Kayla insisted. "Those kids have been through so much already."

"They all have." For the first time Kayla glimpsed compassion. The woman gave a slight shrug. "You might talk to the people in the San Antonio office. They might be able to help you."

Kayla felt a sense of despair. "Where are they?"

The woman found a notepad among the piles of folders on the counter and wrote down the address.

CHAPTER NINE

KAYLA HAD JUST STARTED her car when her cell phone rang. Digging the instrument out of her purse, she checked the screen. Her dad calling from home. She hit a button and put the phone to her ear.

"Good news," he said.

"You found us a tractor." The one he'd checked on the previous week had been too big, and the cultivator that went with it needed too much work.

"Something else."

"Hey," she said, "I'll take whatever I can get."

She hadn't told her father yet about her plans to become a foster parent for Heather and Brad. For one thing, she didn't want him giving her all sorts of reasons why she shouldn't do it. For another, he'd be leaving in a few months, so ultimately the decision wasn't his. Besides, it hadn't been made yet. She was simply exploring the idea.

"I just got off the phone with Mata in Longview," Boyd explained.

Mata Koroniakos owned one of the biggest and most productive vineyards in the Columbia River valley. "She's willing to sell us chardonnay cuttings at a really good price, but she wants me to go and personally take charge of the harvesting and packing."

That relieved Mata of liability if they didn't take, but it was also in Kayla's best interest. There was no one she trusted more to handle this than her father. "When would you have to leave?"

"Right away. Today, in fact, but I don't like leaving you and Megan alone with all the stuff that's going on—"

"Don't worry about us, Dad. We'll be fine."

"Ethan is only a few minutes away. I know he'll help in any way he can."

"We'll be fine," she repeated, remembering her neighbor sitting at their kitchen table two evenings before and the sense of security she felt having him around. Well…maybe more than just a sense of security. The truth was she'd been thinking about his kiss far more than she should.

"There's a flight out of San Antonio in three hours."

"We'd better get moving, then. That's not much time. Confirm your reservations and pack. I'll be home in a few minutes to drive you."

"I hate to put you to all that trouble. I can take my truck and leave it at the airport."

"I need to go to San Antonio anyway. Besides, I might want to use the truck."

He was waiting for her, a small suitcase at his feet, when she pulled up in front of the house. He climbed in without her turning off the engine.

"Considering the price Mata's offering us," he said once they were under way, "I didn't think we'd want to pass this up."

"She has good stock, the best. How long do you expect to be away?"

"Probably not more than four or five days."

Kayla bypassed Loop 1610 on the outskirts of the city and proceeded to the inner ring of Loop 410. Daytime traffic was heavy even between rush hours; fortunately it was moving. She took the exit at McAllister Freeway north to the international airport.

"Call me when you get there," she said, dropping him off at the airline terminal.

"I will."

"And, Dad—thanks."

"No need for that, honey. I love doing it." The smile on his face confirmed it. "Give Megan a great big kiss for me."

"We'll miss you." It was true. She and her dad had always been close but they'd become better friends since her divorce from Daryl. Boyd had been unconditional in his love for her, whether it was marrying a guy he didn't approve of or starting her own vineyard fifteen hundred miles from the only place they'd ever called home.

It took almost half an hour for Kayla to penetrate the heart of San Antonio's commercial district and find parking—four blocks from the address she was looking for.

This CPS office was bigger, but the atmosphere was no warmer. Framed signs on the walls warned of dire consequences for failure to provide accurate information on official documents, followed by lists of applicable state regulations and criminal statutes.

Instead of one woman, however, this office was populated with half a dozen or more workers, all looking harassed, overworked or bored.

A Hispanic woman in her midthirties came up to the counter and brushed back a stray wisp of frizzy red hair that nature had had no part in creating.

"Can I help you?" she asked in a Texas twang.

"I'd like to apply to be a foster parent, Livy," Kayla said, reading the name tag on the woman's blue smock.

Livy walked along the counter gathering papers and forms from beneath it and dropped them in front of Kayla. "Fill these out, being especially careful to answer all the questions in parts two and seven of the personal history statement. You must furnish us with three character references. You'll also have to sign a release for us to access your credit report and any police files."

The stack contained at least twenty pages.

As if reading her mind, Livy added, "You don't have to fill them out right now. Probably don't have all the information with you anyway. Take them home and return them at your convenience. It'll take about six weeks to review your application, assuming we don't have a big backlog. Could be longer then, up to six months. If you're approved, we'll be in touch and set up an interview."

Six weeks just to get an interview? Not encouraging at all.

"Actually, there are two particular children I want to foster."

"Are they currently in the system?"

Kayla explained that they were living with a family in Homestead, but that the foster parents were planning to relocate to another state.

"Well, you can still complete the paperwork," Livy said, "but we won't be able to accept the request for those children until they're released to our jurisdiction."

"But they will be as soon as the Homestead office closes. That's what the woman there told me."

"Could be," Livy admitted. "I don't know anything about that. All I can tell is that those children don't belong to us. Oh, wait, did you say Homestead? Is that your place of residence?"

"Yes, I have a small vin—"

She withdrew the stack of papers, as if they were forbidden candy. "No point in even filling these out, then. Sorry, but you're outside our area."

Kayla could feel her blood pressure rising. This was insane. She was on the verge of arguing with the woman, so she paused and took a deep breath. "I'd like to speak with the head of this office."

Livy eyed her suspiciously, then shrugged. "Sure, but it won't do any good. Her answers'll be the same as mine. She's the one who tells me what to say."

She secreted the papers under the counter, strolled over to a desk in the opposite corner from the one she'd occupied and pointed to Kayla. The other woman nodded, put down her pen and came forward.

"I'm Mrs. Caswell," she told Kayla. "How may I help you?"

Kayla explained the situation.

The woman nodded sympathetically. "Unfortunately there's nothing I can do until the children are actually transferred to our jurisdiction."

Kayla fought to hide her aggravation. "I'm trying to help these children."

Mrs. Caswell sounded genuinely compassionate. "I appreciate that, and believe me, I wish I could accommodate you. I'm not trying to defend the system. Frankly, I think it stinks, but I have to obey the law. I can't accept your application, no matter how much I'd like to. The children don't come under my control, therefore there's nothing I can do about them, either." She shrugged helplessly. "I know how frustrating this is. You sound like just the kind of caring person we're looking for. When the Homestead office is officially closed, and if the children are transferred to this office, I'll be able to determine what's best for them. Until then… I have hundreds of other cases I have to devote myself to."

The woman spoke kindly, diverting Kayla's anger from her to the system they were both stuck with.

"The best advice I can offer at this point is that you keep checking back with us."

"Can I at least fill out the paperwork so it will be on file when that happens?"

Mrs. Caswell considered her question a moment. "I'll give you the paperwork so you can have it ready to turn in as soon as we take over, but I can't accept it or process it until then. You must understand we have lots of people with legitimate applications on file who must be investigated first. I can't tie up resources on a request I know to be invalid."

Kayla felt as if she were caught in a Kafka story.

"Our first concern is, of course, for the children. They'll most likely be transferred here, since we're the largest, closest office, but it's possible Homestead will be annexed to another district."

"Are there no other options?"

The woman considered the question. "The children have no family to take them?"

"The girl's parents were killed in a car accident last summer. She has no one else. The boy... He was taken away from an abusive situation that cost him his right foot."

The woman lowered her eyes and pressed her lips together. "I'm sorry I can't be more helpful."

"Suppose I adopted them," Kayla blurted out.

The woman's brows rose. "You'd be willing to do that?"

"They're good kids. They don't deserve to be bounced around this way."

"None of them do," she said with a flash of genuine anger. "But adoption is a big step, a big responsibility. Are you married? Do you have other children?"

"I'm divorced, but I have full custody of my eight-year-old daughter."

"We prefer married couples. We wouldn't turn down your application, but we'd look at married people first."

"Would the children have any say-so?"

"They're eight and nine? A judge might consider their opinion, but he would have no obligation to honor it. A stable two-parent home is almost always given preference over individuals, unless they're related by blood or marriage."

"But I have a history with them. They know me and my daughter. We're almost like family now."

"That would certainly help, of course, but it's still no guarantee."

Kayla looked at her watch. She'd have to hurry to get home before Megan's bus dropped her off, and the afternoon rush hour was already beginning. She took the application packet and left, more depressed than when she'd entered. Fearful that she might not be able to make it home in time, she used her cell phone to call Ethan.

He answered on the second ring.

"I hate to bother you," she said, "but I'm stuck in San Antonio—"

"What are you doing there?"

"I had to drop my dad at the airport. He's gone to Washington state to get us new stock."

"You work fast." She liked the approval she heard in his voice.

"I should be home in about forty-five minutes, but just in case I'm held up, would you go over and meet Megan? I don't want her to come home to an empty house."

"No trouble at all. I'll bring her over here and give her a riding lesson."

"You're a doll."

"Really?" he asked in amusement.

More than you know, and that makes you even more adorable.

"She'll love that. I'll pay you back somehow, in addition to the fee for the extra lesson, I mean."

"No need for either. I told you, neighbors help neighbors here."

She sighed. "Still, I feel I should do something."

"How about letting me take you out to dinner tonight?"

An image of white linen, sparkling crystal and candlelight came to mind.

"Only if you let me buy." The idea was enticing, but… "Where?" she asked. "What's open at night in Homestead? Besides, I don't have a babysitter for Megan now with Dad gone."

"She can come along."

Kayla was glad he couldn't see her face, because it was hot and probably beet-red. She should be pleased he was including her daughter, but her immediate reaction had been letdown. Even though she wasn't interested in Ethan—she wouldn't allow herself to be interested—as anyone more than a friend and neighbor. Even if he was more a temptation than a doll.

"Oh, okay."

"And since you're buying, you can pick it up on the way home. I had barbecue in mind, but it's your choice. We'll have a picnic. I know the perfect spot."

"Sounds like fun. Give me a little extra time, then, for the food. Say an hour and a half?"

"We'll be here."

They disconnected. A picnic. Well, Megan would enjoy that.

Now the big decision: Barbecued chicken, beef or pork sausage? Megan liked macaroni salad, so she'd get some of that and…

ETHAN LAUGHED as he clicked off his cell phone. He hadn't missed the disappointment in Kayla's voice when she realized he was suggesting a family picnic. He would have liked something more intimate, too, but this wasn't about romance, it was about friendship.

Carter's words came back to him. *She's falling in love with you.*

Worse, he was falling in love with her. He didn't want to be, but he was beyond helping himself when it came to Kayla. They were going to play family tonight. Another mistake. Before this went too far, he would have to pull back. After tonight. He'd already made a commitment. He couldn't renege.

He finished replacing the kick panel in a stall one of his recent boarders had damaged, checked his watch and put his tools away before hopping into his pickup and driving over to Stony Hill. Kayla probably didn't realize all the land she could see from her house had once been part of the Broken Spoke or that he knew every nook and cranny on the place.

Megan was surprised to see him waiting for her when she trudged up the driveway. It took a moment for her to realize something must be wrong.

"Is Mom all right? Where is she? Where's Grandpa? Why are you here?"

"Everything's fine, Megan. Your mom called. She got tied up in San Antonio and your grandpa had to fly to Washington for new grapevines. Your mom asked me to pick you up and take you over to my place. I'll give you an extra riding lesson while we wait for her."

The prospect of riding Birdsong was enticing, but the child was still leery, which he took as a good sign.

"Are you telling the truth?" she asked. "They're both all right? Not like Heather's—"

"She's fine, honey. They both are." He wanted to give her a hug, but he didn't dare. "Tell you what. You know your mom's cell number?"

"Uh-huh."

He removed his phone from the little holster on his belt. "Here, call her and make sure it's okay."

Megan took it, still studying him. He could see she wanted to trust him.

She poked in the numbers. It rang several times before Kayla answered.

"Mom? Is that you?"

Relaxing, Megan started babbling about Ethan being there to pick her up and was it all right for her to go with him. "He wants to give me a special riding lesson on Birdsong. Can I go, Mom, please?" she listened for a few seconds. "Okay. I'll tell him." She disconnected and handed the phone back to him. "She says she'll meet us at the ranch in about half an hour."

"Good. Now, do you need to change clothes?"

Megan used her key and ran inside, leaving the door open. Ethan remained on the small porch and scanned the peaceful landscape he loved.

THEY SAT ON A PLAID wool blanket under a live oak tree on the top of a hill, watching the lowering sun paint the sky in translucent pastels of pink and charcoal, blue and iridescent gold. The wind, so prevalent on the sweeping prairies of Texas, was calm this evening, the air sweet and sultry.

They'd eaten in the shallow valley below, where water bubbled and gurgled up from underground springs to form a lily-covered pool. The soft earth was peppered with the prints of deer and other animals that came to drink.

Megan had been enthralled by the signs of wildlife, especially when Ethan showed her limestone formations imprinted with seashells and mollusks that had thrived here millions of years ago. Now the eight-year-old leaned against a small outcropping, facing the setting sun, her head tilted forward as she slowly succumbed to weariness.

"This all belonged to your family?" Kayla asked.

"Over ten thousand acres at one time. My great-great-grandmother was the one who named it. Have you ever asked yourself why pioneers settled where they did?"

She laughed. "I sure have. Some of the places certainly aren't ones I would have picked."

"The reason we put down roots here probably wasn't much different from a lot of other stories. Dead Mule Ranch was the name of one spread not far from here. That was where a German family was forced to stop when their mule dropped dead in its traces. In our case, it was a broken wagon wheel. While my great-great-grandfather Adolphus Schnorrberger went off in search of a new one, his wife, Hildegard, plunked her bonnet on the limb of a live oak tree and decided she'd gone as far as she was going to. By the time great-great-granddaddy returned with a new wheel, she'd set up camp and started building a house. Supposedly he wanted to name their spread Schnorrberger-viehfarm, but great-great-grandma said that was too much of a mouthful even for a German. She said Der Broken Schpoke was easier."

Kayla laughed. "You made that up—but I love it."

He struggled to maintain a deadpan expression. "They had one child, a daughter. Legend has it the man she married, Gerhardt Ritter, had a gambling problem. One night, after a bout of heavy drinking, he wagered half the ranch in a poker game. The other guy won with four aces."

Her eyes grew wide. "Gallagher?"

He nodded. "The same legend also says Gallagher cheated. Supposedly, when great-great-grandma found out, she took a shotgun to her son-in-law and nearly blew him away. Instead her shot went wild, shattered an oil lamp in the house, and she ended up burning the place down—by accident, of course."

Kayla was trying to decide if she believed any of this. "Colorful people."

"The only good thing about it," Ethan continued, "was that the land my great-grandfather gave up was downstream from the springs, so at least we still had plenty of water. More hard times followed, though, and over the years the family had to sell off chunks of the place. We were down to a little over a thousand acres by the time my parents got married."

"That's still a lot of land."

"The other two big landowners were Clint Gallagher, who'd inherited the Four Aces, and Clyde Braxton, who'd bought the K-bar-C, which was our last big sale during the Depression. Dad had been hoping to buy the spread back when the old man died. The problem was we were cash poor, so Dad got together with other ranchers and talked them into forming a consortium to raise the money to purchase the place. He hoped to be able to buy them out a few years down the road."

"What about your mom?" Kayla asked. "How did she feel about it?"

Ethan didn't remember any of the details of the discussions between his parents, only that his dad had been positive and hopeful.

"She was by nature more cautious, asked a lot of questions, but when decision time came she bowed to his judgment."

"She disagreed with him?"

"I think she had reservations, but if she had really been against the plan, Dad wouldn't have gone through with it."

"Then the consortium collapsed."

"I was just about to graduate from A&M when my sister died. Angela had been sick for years, and even though we knew the end was inevitable, my mother withdrew from everyone, even my dad, after that. I came home after college, but there wasn't much I could do—for her or for the ranch."

"I'm sorry," Kayla said. "It must have been heartbreaking."

He shook his head slowly. "It was like we were bit players in a story someone else had written."

She reached over and clasped his hand.

"My mother died a year after my sister. Heart failure. She went to bed one night and didn't wake up."

Millicent said Valerie had died of a broken heart. Kayla could imagine it was true.

"Dad never recovered from their deaths."

The silence between them lingered for several minutes. The sky was darkening.

Ethan nodded toward Megan, who was sound asleep. "She's had a busy day."

"Oh, dear. I'll have to wake her."

"I can carry her."

He went over and carefully lifted the child, cushioning her head against his shoulder. She stirred for a moment, then put her arms around his neck, snuggled against him and closed her eyes.

Kayla picked up the blanket and trekked alongside him. It was a strange feeling, the two of them and the sleeping child. Strange and frighteningly wonderful.

The walk back to Kayla's house seemed longer, slower without the excited girl running ahead of them, yet Ethan didn't want the journey to end.

Inside, he laid her on her bed, helped remove her shoes and socks, then left the room while Kayla finished and tucked her in.

"Thank you," she whispered as she carefully pulled the bedroom door to, leaving it open just a crack. "Will you stay a few minutes? You must be thirsty."

This is a mistake, he told himself. "Thanks."

They sat in the living room, each with soft drinks. "You obviously love kids, yet you told me you have no intention of ever getting married. Am I being too nosy if I ask why?"

He pursed his lips, as a shadow seemed to pass across his face. "You know I had a younger sister, Angela, who died."

She nodded. "I'm sorry."

"Do you know how?"

"I heard she got lead poisoning from eating Mexican candy."

"I was the one who gave her the candy, Kayla. I killed her."

CHAPTER TEN

KAYLA DIDN'T KNOW HOW to react, what to say. All she could see was the forlorn expression on Ethan's face, the dead look in his eyes. He'd been carrying this guilt around for years. A heavy burden.

"You didn't kill her," she insisted, "even if you did give her the candy. You certainly didn't intend her harm."

His laugh was mirthless. "My intent doesn't change what happened."

"You honestly blame yourself for her illness and death?"

"I gave her the candy behind my parents' back because I knew they didn't approve. If I'd obeyed them, she wouldn't have eaten it and wouldn't have gotten sick. Of course I'm responsible for her death."

Putting her hand on his forearm, aware of his wire-taut muscles, she looked directly into his eyes.

"You're smarter than that, Ethan."

He pulled away. "It's late." He started to rise from the couch. "I'd better get going. We both have work to do tomorrow."

"Don't go." She clasped his arm again. "Please, don't go. Let's talk."

"There's nothing to talk about." But he made no further effort to rise. "What are you, a shrink now?"

"Tell me what happened."

He hesitated, gazed at her, lifted his shoulders and settled back against the couch.

"I'd just turned fourteen when I started high school and was feeling pretty smug about myself. I'd made the football team. Pablo García was on the team, too. His mom was American, but his dad was from Mexico. He used to drive down to Monterey every six weeks or so to visit his mother. On one of his trips he brought back tamarind candy for Pablo, who gave me some."

Ethan upended the already empty soft drink can he'd previously abandoned.

Kayla wondered if it was safe to offer him another. An interruption in the tempo of his narrative now might break the spell. Yet intuition told her he needed to get this out, that having started, nothing could stop him.

"I'll get you another soda." She disappeared

into the kitchen and returned seconds later with a fresh can.

"Thanks." He looked up and met her eyes for the first time. She wasn't sure if the gratitude she saw there was for the drink or her willingness to listen. The aluminum can clicked and hissed when he pulled the tab.

"I gave Angela some of the candy when I got home. My mother caught us and told Angela she could have that piece but didn't want her eating a lot of junk. She warned me I'd better lay off it, too, if I didn't want zits." He sniffed. "I gave Angela the rest of what I had and told her not to let Mom catch her with it."

He sipped his soda. "When I saw Pablo again, I told him my kid sister really liked the candy. So on his next trip, Mr. García brought me a great big bag and I gave it to Angela. After that, every time he went home, Pablo's dad brought back another sack. I'd eat a piece or two, but Angela devoured the stuff."

He took another sip of soda and put the can down.

"Toward the end of my second year, Luella found Angela's latest stash and went ballistic. I couldn't imagine why she was so mad. It was just candy."

He took a deep breath. "It turned out she'd

read an article in one of her Spanish magazines a few days earlier about Mexican candy being tainted with all sorts of stuff, ranging from unacceptable levels of fecal matter to toxic chemicals. Did you know there are acceptable levels of fecal matter?"

He frowned. "Well, my parents went berserk when Luella told them. My mother had just heard about kids in Oklahoma getting lead poisoning from eating tamarind candy made in Mexico. Angela and I were tested. They found trace amounts of lead in my system, but Angela, who was six years younger, had a lot more in hers."

Kayla watched his hands tighten into fists. She doubted he was even aware of it.

"We both underwent chelation. When it was over I was given a clean bill of health. Well, almost. Angela… She'd eaten so much of it… They were able to remove a lot of the lead from her bloodstream, but her organs had already been affected."

When he lifted his eyes, they were glassy, and the expression on his face was one of agony. "It took her six years to die, Kayla…." He took a ragged breath. "All because I gave her candy."

Kayla took his fisted hand and spread the fingers, forcing him to release the tension.

"In the end it killed my mother and father, too." He withdrew his hand and stood.

"So now you know why I'll never marry," he concluded, "why I'll never have children. After the chelation, the doctor told me my blood tests all came out clean, but that he couldn't guarantee my DNA hadn't been irreparably damaged. There was a possibility I could produce defective children, so I had a vasectomy the day after I turned eighteen. I won't marry, either. I destroyed one family. I can't be responsible for destroying another."

Kayla ached for him. He was carrying guilt that no man should have to bear. His culpability was unreasonable, yet she couldn't fault his logic.

She felt so helpless. There were no magic words to make the pain go away.

ETHAN RETURNED HOME in a funk deeper than he'd suffered since he'd found his father's body, the gun still warm in his hand. Another of a long series of tragedies he'd caused. Sometimes he wondered if his father hadn't had the right idea. Living with the shame and guilt were at times a burden he didn't think he could bear, yet his body went on.

He hadn't missed the compassion or the pity in Kayla's eyes as he'd told her his story. Ironic laughter stirred inside him. Till then she'd thought she was falling in love with him. He'd seen that in her eyes, too. Earlier. In the moments when she thought he wasn't looking.

He should be flattered, delighted—reach out and grasp what she wanted to give him. But he'd made a vow, and no matter how much he wanted Kayla, he couldn't have her. He'd done enough harm; he wouldn't do more. Getting involved would only hurt them both.

KAYLA SPENT THE NEXT two days tearing out dead and dying grapevines. The cover crops of clover, mustard and lavender she'd planted to enrich the soil had also been destroyed, so it all had to be plowed under. At least it would add compost to help aerate the soil.

The work was backbreaking, digging out old plants, untwisting new sprouts from the wires they'd so carefully strung. Tilling and turning the dirt, and the inevitable cleanup. By the time Megan and her friends got off the school bus Wednesday afternoon, Kayla was exhausted. Her back ached, her muscles screamed. Taking the kids over to Ethan's was a treat, if only because it allowed her to sit still for a few minutes.

"Mommy, I need another inhaler," Megan announced as she changed into her riding clothes.

She seemed to be going through a lot of inhalers lately, more than usual, but then, this was early spring, a time of year that was always a challenge.

"There's an extra one in my medicine cabinet," Kayla responded. "I'll get it. Mark it on the shopping list in the kitchen, will you please, and I'll pick up more at the drugstore tomorrow. After your lesson this afternoon, I also want you to use the nebulizer."

"Can we have sloppy joes for supper tonight?"

Kayla smiled. Sloppy joes were one of Megan's favorites, but since Grandpa hated them, the only time they indulged now was when he wasn't around. "You're on."

"Can Heather and Brad eat with us?"

They were sitting out on the front porch. Her friends probably had a lot of sloppy joes at the Rayborn house. Kayla was about to suggest another time, then thought of something. "Did you tell them you were going to ask me if they could stay?"

"Uh-huh. I told them you make the best sloppy joes in the whole wide world."

Her father would say there wasn't much difference between the worst and the best. In this case, though, the point wasn't the food but the company.

"Okay—" she held up her hand as Megan started to bolt down the porch steps to tell them "—but next time ask me before you talk to them. It wouldn't be nice to build up their expectations if for some reason they couldn't stay. I also have to call Mrs. Rayborn to make sure it's all right with her. Do you understand?"

Megan nodded.

A few minutes later, the four of them piled out of Kayla's Toyota at the Broken Spoke.

Ethan was in the ring riding Duke when they arrived. He'd done miracles with the skittish young horse. As the kids watched, he brought the gelding down from a light trot to an extended walk, circled twice and dismounted.

Kayla saw him now in a different light. He was no longer just a good-looking horseman who contributed precious time to handicapped children, but a man trying to atone for an unforgivable sin.

His eyes, when they met hers, betrayed him,

though. As casual as he was trying to be today, it was a facade.

After introducing the kids to a couple of new maneuvers, their fifth therapeutic riding candidate arrived. A four-year-old boy who had been born with severe fetal alcohol syndrome. His facial features were bland, immature, almost as if he had Down's. His speech was limited. According to the report Ethan had received, Norbert was also prone to temper tantrums. Because he was small for his age and had balance problems, Ethan elected to ride bareback with him, as he had with Daphne.

Norbert was at first nervous around the big animal, but petting Birdsong calmed him quickly. When he clapped the horse in the muzzle, Ethan wasn't sure if it was a spasm or intentional. Fortunately it wasn't with enough force to provoke the patient old mare, but when Ethan pulled the boy away, it brought on a tantrum. The boy's grandmother, who had permanent custody of her alcoholic daughter's child, had warned Ethan of his strength, but as he struggled with the boy, he realized he hadn't given the elderly woman enough credit. How did she cope with him by herself?

After a time-out, Ethan mounted Birdsong from the block and lifted the boy onto the horse and sat him in front of him. The slow ride began. By the second circuit, the youngster had calmed down and was relaxed against Ethan's chest. They rode for more than twenty minutes. When Ethan lifted him off the mare, the boy was grinning.

"Say thank you," his grandmother prompted him as she straightened his clothes and kissed him on the cheek.

Norbert looked up at Ethan, a smile on his lips. "Fank ou."

"You're welcome."

"Can I bring him back?" the grandmother asked, clearly worried that the earlier episode may have discouraged Ethan.

"You bet." He looked down at the small child. "We're going to have a good time riding together, aren't we?"

The boy nodded, grinning.

"Thank you." The woman's eyes were moist.

"One more to evaluate," Ethan said to Kayla after the other two were gone.

KAYLA WAITED until after lunch Thursday, when the children were still in school, to drop by and see Leona Rayborn.

"I heard you'll be leaving, going to Chicago."

Leona had invited Kayla in, closing the door

behind her. She held the infant, a dish towel on her shoulder to catch dribbles.

"Randy's got a job lined up with a shipping company up there," she said quietly. "Not much work around here."

Leona cradled the baby's head with her free hand. "We're just scraping by on the allowance we get for the six kids I take care of here. Up there we can do better, maybe even with only four or five."

"Cost of living's higher, though," Kayla commented.

"Yeah, and there's a lot more to spend it on, but if Randy actually lands this job, we should do all right."

"What about the kids you have here?"

Leona paced the shabby living room. "What about them?"

"I mean, what will happen to them?"

"Somebody else'll take care of them. I hope they get good families. The stories you hear about what happens in some foster homes is enough to make your blood boil." She looked sideways at Kayla. "You think I'm just in this for the money, don't you?"

Before Kayla could defend herself, the woman went on. "You're partially right. If I didn't make money at it, I probably wouldn't do it. I don't get real close to any of the kids, because I know they're going to be leaving—maybe tomorrow, maybe a couple of years from now, but one way or another, they'll be gone from my life."

She laid the now-sleeping child in a crib next to a mock fireplace. "But let me tell you something, I take good care of these kids. Do I love them?" She paused, the question clearly rhetorical, one she alone could answer. After a moment she said angrily, "I don't dare or they'll tear my heart out." She took a breath. "But they don't go wanting, either."

"I didn't mean—"

"Yes, you did." Leona covered the sleeping tyke with a flannel blanket and removed a half-empty bottle of juice. "I don't blame you."

She walked toward the kitchen, her demeanor less defiant, less defensive. "These kids deserve more, but the truth is I can't give it. I wanted kids of my own when we got married, before I found out I couldn't have any. So now I take care of other people's throwaways. Wish I could love them, but it would just mean more heartache if I did. So I take care of them the best I can. A job, I guess you would call it, but it's a twenty-four-hour-a-day job. This is what I do."

"I'm sorry," Kayla said, suddenly aware that the other woman was close to tears.

Leona waved the sympathy away. "You're worried about Heather and Brad? I don't blame you. They're good kids, really."

"I tried to apply to be their foster mother—" Kayla started to explain.

Leona snickered. "But you ran into the bureaucracy, right?"

Kayla nodded. "One office won't talk to me because they're closing. The other won't have anything to do with me because I'm outside their jurisdiction."

"Yeah, it's known as falling through the cracks. About the only thing that'll save those kids from being bounced from pillar to post is adoption. You married?"

"Divorced."

"Cuts your chances, then. They want perfect two-parent families. Your ex still in the picture?"

"No."

"That's good. Less messy. Won't have to worry about one kid going off to be with Daddy while the others stay home with you. Rough situation, that. You receiving child support?"

She'd been granted child support in her divorce, but Daryl had rarely come through with it. She was even less likely to get payments now that he'd taken a job overseas and she'd moved to Texas—she hadn't so far—but she could live with that. She wished Megan had a father in her life, but Kayla had seen what Daryl's erratic visits did to her daughter's health.

"Nothing I can rely on," Kayla said.

"That's not so good, unless you're independently wealthy."

Kayla laughed. "Hardly."

"Work full-time, then?"

"I'm starting a vineyard," she said proudly. "Believe me, it's a full-time job right now. I plan to get my teaching certificate this summer and substitute next year."

"That won't help, and I wouldn't go around bragging about it, either. Single woman, running her own business, working a second job? They'll say you're too busy to be anything but a part-time mom."

Kayla was aghast. "You mean they'd rather let those kids be bounced from foster home to foster home than have a single parent adopt them?"

Leona shrugged. "I'm just saying it would be a lot easier if you were married and only one of you was working, or if you were just working part-time at home."

These weren't the answers Kayla wanted to hear. "When do you move?"

"About six weeks, but it may be sooner if Randy's job comes through before then."

"Do the children know about this?"

Leona shook her head. "It'll be tough enough on them when it happens. No use upsetting them yet."

Kayla was sure Heather and Brad didn't know, because they would have said something to her. "Will you call me when you find out?"

The other woman nodded. "As soon as I know anything for sure."

THE LAST CHILD Noah had on his list was Tabitha Sinclair, who had Down syndrome. The oldest of the group, Tabby was twelve, big and chubby for her age.

When Ethan introduced her to Birdsong, her trepidation quickly vanished. She would have been content to continue petting the animal interminably if Ethan and Birdsong had let her.

Getting her up on the horse took longer than it had with the other children. The girl was leery of the mounting block's tall steps and frightened about reaching across the gap to the horn of the big Western saddle. Ethan got on the horse twice to show her how easy it was, and after much persuasion, with his hands supporting her waist, she practically leaped the narrow distance.

Ethan walked her for about fifteen minutes, first in one direction, then in the other. But when he wanted to end the session, she objected vehemently. Yet the child was unused to this type of exercise and would undoubtedly be sore the following day. Her mother had also told him Tabitha would let the lesson go on forever, that getting her off later would be just as difficult. Discipline and structure were important in the girl's life. Sending the wrong message on this first visit would be hard to overcome later. After repeated promises from both Ethan and her mother, the girl finally dismounted. They left with the understanding that she could return.

As Ethan and Kayla were leading Birdsong to the stable for the night, he asked, "So what do you think of our lineup?"

"The children obviously love it, and you do a terrific job with them."

"May I remind you," he said with a thin smile, "we're in this together. I took the job on the condition that you help." He didn't tell her he was willing to go on without her.

"Working with these kids on a permanent

basis will mean a commitment of time and energy," he continued. "Between your vineyard and taking care of Megan, you already have a pretty heavy load."

"It won't take much more time than it is already," she pointed out. "Or am I missing something?"

He grinned at her and was still smiling when he asked, "Do you seriously think those six kids are the only ones with special needs in this community? Once we agree to work with the children in Noah's congregation, we'll be inundated with other requests."

"I hadn't thought about that."

"That's why I hesitated."

She considered him a minute. "You'll do it regardless of what I say, won't you?"

He blinked. She'd caught him. "I don't see how I can say no. Do you?"

"I'm sorry, Ethan. I shouldn't have gotten you roped into this. It was unfair of me, putting you in this spot."

"You didn't see where it would lead. That's nothing for you to blame yourself for."

Like giving candy to a kid sister. Didn't he realize what he was saying? That there are times when we have to be judged on our intentions, not their results.

"What do you want to do?" she asked.

"Two things." He'd obviously thought this through, making her even more aware of how shortsighted she'd been. "First, we need to look into formal training on dealing with kids with special needs. There's an international organization that specializes in it."

She nodded. "PATH. But that'll take time and money."

"That's the second thing," he said. "Since Noah instigated this, I think we should put him in charge of enrolling volunteers and raising whatever funds it'll take to get people properly trained."

Clever. She grinned. "You're absolutely right. If you like, I'll talk to him about it when I see him on Sunday. Unless," she added, "you want to come to church with us."

"Thanks, but I'll pass. Maybe another time."

CHAPTER ELEVEN

AT CHURCH ON SUNDAY THE parents of the special-needs children who'd been out to the Broken Spoke during the week thanked Kayla profusely for her help. The kids were still talking about their riding lessons.

"What you and Ethan are doing is terrific," Shawna Jones said, speaking for the others. "By the way, where is he?"

Kayla was a bit thrown by the question. She wasn't his keeper, but people were talking to her—about them—as if they were a pair. She'd have to disabuse them of that notion quickly, because sharing coffee at her kitchen table and working side by side in the riding arena didn't make them a pair, a couple of kisses notwithstanding. He'd made that abundantly clear, and she hadn't forgotten his Saturday night on the town.

"I have no idea," she said. "I only see him on riding days." *Or when someone poisons my vineyard and I need him to play confidant, ad-*

visor and available shoulder to cry on. "He's pretty busy the rest of the time with his horses."

She received sage nods as people excused themselves and wandered to their vehicles to go home to Sunday dinners with their families.

Noah finally broke away from the people he was talking to and came over to greet Kayla. He listened to her talk about the kids they'd evaluated at the Broken Spoke. Then she reported the conditions Ethan had levied on continuing the program.

"I'll gladly get volunteers to help you, and I'll raise the necessary funds. That's the least I can do."

He also agreed with Ethan's assessment that there would probably be a few more families throughout Loveless County coming forward once word got out.

"He's absolutely wonderful with children," Kayla commented. "Infinitely patient and caring."

Noah nodded thoughtfully. "You know his background…?"

"About his sister? Yes, he's told me all about the candy…."

He seemed surprised. "The old-timers in town know what happened, but I don't think he's ever discussed it with anyone. I'm glad to hear you're getting him to open up. Sounds like the two of you are good for each other."

Each other? What had he done for her, other than make her want things she no longer had a right to?

Noah smiled, as if he were reading her mind. "He's good for you, too, and for your daughter. I can see it in your eyes."

Kayla felt heat flood her cheeks. She looked away, embarrassed. Was she that transparent? Was everyone smiling behind her back, snickering?

"I'll get busy on this right away." Noah was clearly trying to defuse the tension that had crept between them. "I have several people in mind who'll be glad to help out and a few contacts I'm sure will want to contribute to the cause. Give me a few days to get back to you with names."

She smiled. "Thank you, Noah."

On her way home, Kayla's mind fumbled with the ideas going through her head. Her determination began to falter. What she was about to propose was daring, outrageous and scary, but she didn't see any other option. Ethan would probably reject the idea out of hand. He had every right to. He'd already made his position clear, but this was about the children, not about him or her.

He was riding an unfamiliar mare in the big arena when she pulled up at the side of the barn. She'd stopped at home first to change into jeans. Leaning on the pipe fence next to the gate, she watched him put the horse through its paces, circles and diagonals at a walk, trot, lope. The mare responded superbly, at least to her untrained eye. Of course Kayla was more focused on the rider than the horse, so maybe she was missing something.

He brought the horse to a leisurely walk and came over to where she was standing. "Where's Megan?" he asked from the saddle.

Kayla had to crane her neck to look up at him. The man was impressive from any angle, but from this vantage point she got a particularly fascinating glimpse of muscular legs, wide shoulders and broad chest.

"Invited to a birthday party at a girlfriend's house."

She paralleled him on her side of the fence as he walked the pewter-gray horse toward the gate, where he dismounted and removed the saddle. Draping it over the top rail, he replaced the tack and bit with a halter. Kayla followed as he led the bright-eyed mare to the pasture and set her free to join her sisters.

"So how did it go with Noah?" he asked. They turned back toward the barn. He grabbed the heavy saddle on the way. She carried the bridle.

She told him, leaving out Noah's observation that they were good for each other. "He'll call this week and let me know who's available to help out. He also promised to start raising funds."

"Good."

She held her breath a minute, then steeled herself. "There's something else I'd like to talk to you about."

He paused in lifting the silver-trimmed Western saddle onto its rack and glanced over his shoulder at her. "A problem?"

She nodded. "The Rayborns are moving out of state."

He relieved her of the bridle, which he hung on its hook. "So the kids will have to go to another foster home. From what you've told me the Rayborns aren't the most loving couple, anyway." He shook his head. "Sure makes their lives unstable, though." He pulled back and stared at her. "They won't be split up, will they? Those two are like brother and sister."

"It gets worse," Kayla said. "The local CPS office is closing in about six weeks. All the children under their jurisdiction will be transferred to the San Antonio district."

"Okay," he said tentatively, obviously aware there was more to the story. Then it struck him. "You're not telling me they'll be relocated away from here?"

She nodded.

He muttered a word she hadn't heard him use before. She completely agreed with his assessment.

"Surely—"

She told him about applying to be a foster parent and the runaround she'd received at the two offices. "It's like trying to fight the wind."

He flexed his jaw, the muscle play downright distracting.

"I had a long talk with Leona," Kayla went on. "She probably knows the system as well as anybody, and she wasn't very encouraging. She did hold out one hope, though."

He let out a breath and shifted his weight to his right hip. "What's that?"

"Adopt them."

He stared at her for what seemed an eternity. "You want to adopt Heather and Brad? That's an awfully big step, Kayla. Two more children.

They're great kids, and I know you'd be an absolutely wonderful mother to them, but that's an enormous responsibility. Are you sure you want to do that?"

"Would you adopt them if you could?"

He shook his head. "For me it's not an option. The establishment would never allow a single man to adopt kids their ages. Not with all the scandals these past few years."

"But would you if you could?"

He studied her, then waved his hand dismissively. "It's a moot point, Kayla. I have three strikes against me. I'm a single male. I have no family to integrate them into, not to mention my remote location, and my past history with my sister doesn't recommend me."

He was right on the first count, had a point on the second, but she wanted to argue the third. The expression on his face and the determination in his voice, however, told her it was a lost cause. He'd had years to exonerate himself of his sister's fate, but he still hadn't found absolution. Noah had mentioned that Ethan never talked about the tragedy of his sister's illness and death. Had he ever received counseling of any kind? She doubted it. Given his father's ultimate choice, she doubted Ritter men were the type who sought or accepted that kind of help.

"You may be right." She sounded discouraged. "I'd adopt them by myself, except it seems my chances aren't much better than yours. I'm a divorced woman with a chronically ill daughter, receiving no child support and trying to establish a new business that's just been destroyed by a vandal. Those are the strikes against me."

"I'd call that a slight exaggeration," he said with what looked like a smile. "You're a great mom with expert credentials in a growing industry, and you're not letting a setback stop you from achieving your goal."

The sincerity in his eyes told her he believed every word. It brought warmth, not for the compliment as much as the realization that he respected, even admired her.

"I like your version better," she admitted, returning his wan smile, "but I have to be realistic. The people who administer these programs are conditioned to say no." She eyed him, unsure whether she dared bring up her next point. "There is one possible way we can save them."

He leaned against the half door of a stall and crossed his arms. Did he have any idea how attractive he looked? But of course he didn't, and that just made him more appealing.

"What's that?" he asked.

"You and I could get married."

He bolted up straight. "What?"

His shock instinctively made her take a step back.

"You must be out of your mind. I already told you—"

"Let me explain."

He strode down the central alley. She had to trot to keep up. "You're being ridiculous, Kayla. Stupid."

"Ethan, listen—"

He spun to face her, his features dark, eyes narrowed, as hard and impenetrable as jade. "No, Kayla, you listen. You of all people... I told you about... I've made my position clear. No marriage. No children." He stomped back toward the feed room.

"Ethan," she called out, rushing to catch up with him. "Ethan, calm down and let me explain." She grabbed him by the arm, stopping him, but he refused to look at her. Tension cascaded off him in waves.

"When I'm finished," she said, "all you have to do is say yes or no."

He closed his eyes. "I've already said no."

"What I'm suggesting," she persisted, "is a marriage of convenience. We go through a quiet civil ceremony and immediately petition to adopt Heather and Brad. Once the adoption is complete and they're legally ours, we just as quietly divorce. All our properties will remain in our own names and we still maintain separate bank accounts, so there won't be any problem about dividing up assets when we divorce. I'll take the kids. I'll even sign a prenuptial agreement, promising not to ask for child support. You won't have any financial obligations toward me or them."

He gaped at her. "You've got it all worked out, haven't you?" he practically growled through clenched teeth.

"I think so," she said, pretending she wasn't aware of his sarcasm.

"Well, there are just a few minor details you failed to consider—aside from the fact that you're asking me to commit fraud."

He began to pace. "Even if we were to get married tomorrow, we wouldn't be able to prevent Child Protective Services from relocating those kids. They'd yank Heather and Brad out of here, and we couldn't even offer them the consolation of knowing it's only until we can adopt them, because that would give them false hope. We have no idea if our application for adoption will be approved, or how long the whole bureaucratic process will take. And if we failed to adopt them, it would be even more devastating for them."

He stopped, his head bowed.

"There's no way I'd bring children into my home and then walk out on them. Just because your husband did that doesn't mean I can or will. Divorce would tear those kids apart. They'd blame themselves.

"Besides," he said, straightening, "I could not, would not, ever walk away from my financial obligations toward them. If I were to adopt them, they would be my children, not playthings to be shuffled—"

"Okay. Stop." Kayla turned away, unwilling to let him see the tears stinging her eyes. "I just thought... Forget it."

ETHAN WATCHED HER rip out of the courtyard, down the long drive and disappear from view. She'd been crying, though she'd made a valiant attempt to hide it from him.

He was furious. Who did he think he was playing the holier-than-thou role? He had absolutely no right to preach to her about anything. Her proposal had been shocking, but the real reason for his anger was that he wanted to accept it.

Did she have any idea what it would be like

for him, to be that close to her and not be able to hold her, kiss her?

Her suggestion had staggered him. She was willing to go that far to save the children from being lost in the system?

For all his posturing, he'd been right. Marrying under those conditions would be wrong and ultimately do more harm than good. Unless…she grew to love him. But why should she? How could she? She knew what he'd done, the legacy of death that trailed him.

His sanctimoniousness didn't make the problem go away, so what were they going to do about the children?

He kept going back to their kisses and what it felt like to have Kayla in his arms. The look in her eyes that said she wanted to be close to him.

BOYD CALLED KAYLA from Longview Sunday evening. He'd supervised the selection and packing of five thousand prime cuttings and sounded happy.

"When will you be home?" She wondered what he would think of the proposal she'd made to Ethan. Misguided, probably.

"The truck left this afternoon. I tried to get a flight out of here tomorrow, but everything's booked, so I won't be leaving until Tuesday morning with a long layover in L.A. I don't get into San Antonio until just after five, smack-dab in the middle of rush hour. Really messes up your schedule. Sorry."

"We'll be glad to have you home," she assured him. "I'll bring Megan with me."

"Any new developments on the poisoning?"

"The sheriff called me yesterday to say he's widening the search of possible sources of the herbicide. He checked locally and in San Antonio, but no one has sold any large quantities in the past six months. He's checking Austin now."

"Had to buy it somewhere. I suppose they could have made a lot of small purchases."

"That's what Wade thinks. Probably paid cash at a bunch of different outlets, so there won't be any records."

"Time consuming," Boyd said, "but it leaves no doubt about premeditation. What's the status of the security system?"

"The big outfit that handles Gallagher's ranch offered to put me on a waiting list to do a survey a month from now. I told them I couldn't wait that long. The other one came out Friday afternoon. I'm going with them."

"Was Ethan there when you met with them?"

For a moment Kayla wanted to protest that

she didn't need a man to make a decision for her, but her father was probably asking because Ethan had offered to be backup.

"With *her*," she corrected. "The rep was a retired female cop from Houston. Yeah, I called Ethan and he came over."

"When will they do the installation?"

"Tomorrow and Tuesday. If all goes well, it'll be up Tuesday night."

"Good timing, then, since the cuttings should arrive that afternoon. How's Megan?"

"Fine. She's really excited to be in the school pageant."

"That's great. No problems otherwise?"

Kayla knew he was referring to his granddaughter's asthma. "A little bit of congestion on Friday, but it's probably just spring pollen."

"Keep her indoors."

Kayla laughed. "Easier said than done. I wish I could bottle her energy. Except for her lessons on Birdsong, though, I do keep her inside as much as possible."

"See you Tuesday at five, then."

"Be safe, Dad."

KAYLA RECEIVED a fax of the report from the lab in Oregon Monday at noon, confirming what she already knew, that herbicide had killed her vineyard. Specifically, Roundup.

"At least now we have it in writing from a recognized authority," Sheriff Montgomery said when she called him.

"Unfortunately this doesn't also tell us who did it or why."

"Anything else that might give us a clue?"

"I don't know how significant this may be," she replied, "but there's a note that the concentration of the chemical was markedly stronger than recommended."

"Hmm. Does that mean whoever used it was unfamiliar with the product?"

"Definitely overkill. Even a slightly weakened solution would have been enough to destroy these vulnerable young sprouts. So why increase the dosage?"

"To be sure it worked?" he asked.

"Or, it could indicate the user doesn't know anything about budding plants."

"In other words, not a farmer."

"Or a gardener."

The whole situation was depressing, Kayla thought as she hung up. Someone was trying to put her out of business before she really got started. The foster children were being transferred out of the district, perhaps never to return. Then there was the constant push-pull she felt with Ethan.

To make matters even worse, Megan had been stuffed-up Monday morning. It didn't appear to be anything serious, but with an asthmatic any respiratory distress could become life-threatening.

Kayla put her on the nebulizer and was tempted to keep her home for the day, but Megan insisted on going to school because they were rehearsing for the spring pageant, and the little ham—Kayla had to smile at her daughter's instinct for dramatics—didn't want to miss anything, especially since she had a starring roll.

Megan was having more difficulty breathing when she came home on the school bus that afternoon with Heather and Brad. There was no way, however, that Kayla would take her daughter over to the Broken Spoke. She hadn't shown particular sensitivity to horses but a combination of otherwise innocuous elements could trigger a severe reaction or make a mild one worse.

It didn't seem fair to deprive the other two of their favorite diversion because Megan couldn't go.

She called Ethan and explained the situation.

"Luella sneezes like crazy this time of year," he said. "A lot of ragweed and wild mustard in bloom now. Best thing is to keep her indoors. As for Heather and Brad, I'll come over and pick them up, then take them home afterward."

"I hate to put you to all that trouble."

"It's no trouble," he said.

There was a pause before he disconnected, as if he had more to say. She hung up the phone with a feeling of dissatisfaction.

He arrived a few minutes later, honked the horn and waited in the truck with the engine running. The children bolted out the door to meet him, Kayla trailing behind.

She'd lain awake most of the night reliving the conversation they'd had in the barn, seeing the wounded look in his eyes. Would he ever forgive her?

"Thanks for doing this," she said through his open window.

"Sure," he replied casually. "I would've come inside except I reek of horse sweat, and I didn't know if that might affect Megan. How's she doing?"

"I have her on the nebulizer again. That should help. If it doesn't, I'll have to take her in to the clinic."

"Call me if you do. I promise to even take

a shower and put on clean clothes first." He grinned.

She almost wished he wouldn't. There was mischief in his eyes, as well as concern. A deadly combination. Did this mean he'd forgiven her?

"I was going to talk to you about your odor," she mumbled.

His eyes widened and he sniffed. "That bad, huh?"

She laughed. "Beat it, before Megan comes charging out and tries to tag along."

She watched his crew cab pull down the driveway and waved back at the kids buckled in the backseat.

CHAPTER TWELVE

THE FIRST THING KAYLA noticed when Megan got off the school bus Tuesday was that she didn't run up to the house, and her mother's instinct immediately went into overdrive. Megan was a natural barrel of energy, always on the go, rarely slowing down until she went to bed at night. But now her daughter was trudging up the driveway like an old woman.

"Have you been using your inhaler?"

"Yes, Mommy," Megan wheezed as she crossed the threshold into the house.

Kayla knelt in front of her for a quick examination. Red eyes, runny nose. Her breathing was too fast, labored. "Come on, let's get you on the nebulizer."

Megan didn't argue, a sure sign she wasn't feeling well.

In Megan's bedroom, Kayla turned on the little oxygen generator and put drops of albuterol sulfate mixed with ipratropium into the atomizer of the long plastic tube. Megan sat in the small padded chair across from her frilly four-poster. As the machine chugged and gurgled, Megan sucked the wispy vapor through her mouth.

"Better?" Kayla asked when she turned it off ten minutes later.

Megan took a deeper breath. "Yes, Mommy." She was breathing more easily, but was still lethargic.

"You can rest in the car on the drive to San Antonio to pick up Grandpa."

"Will we see the Alamo again?" Megan had been fascinated by the place when they visited it soon after their arrival in Texas.

"Not today, honey. The Alamo is downtown, a long way from the airport."

She locked the house as they left.

"Can we have Mexican food while we're there?" Megan asked. "Sara Gallagher at school says they have the best Mexican food on the Riverwalk. Can we go there?"

"Not this trip, sweetheart. That's downtown, too." Okay, she was hungry, so she must be feeling better. "We're just going to pick up Grandpa and come right back."

"I promised Ethan I'd clean Birdsong's stall today."

"That's okay. I called him earlier and let him know you wouldn't be coming over."

Actually she'd left the message on his voice mail, relieved when she got it instead of having to talk to him. He'd been pleasant yesterday, but that had been with the kids around. She still wasn't sure how he felt.

"But Birdsong will miss me."

Kayla's heart felt weighed down. Megan loved that old mare, and caring for her had been good for the child. Kayla would have to make sure her relationship with Ethan didn't deteriorate to the point where she couldn't go over there—for Megan's sake, and for the handicapped kids they were supposed to help together.

"I'm sure Birdsong will understand. It's not like she'll be with strangers. Ethan's been feeding and grooming her for a long time."

"She likes Ethan," Megan said. "I do, too."

The child didn't say it, but Kayla could hear the unspoken words. *I wish he was my daddy.*

She mentioned her father very little since they'd moved to Texas. Daryl had never been an ideal parent, cuddling and tickling one minute, stern and remote the next. The mood swings often left Megan confused and worried.

The fights he and Kayla had had after he'd lost his job had caused Megan her most severe asthma attacks.

All that was over now. He was out of their lives, and Megan had been physically and emotionally healthier ever since. Kayla could credit her father for the stability he brought to their lives. He was a good grandparent, but like so many men of his generation, he wasn't emotionally demonstrative. Ethan, on the other hand, had no hesitation about giving Megan a hug when she needed it. Ironic, considering his renunciation of marriage and family.

Boyd greeted them with open arms, giving Megan a brief embrace and Kayla a paternal kiss on the cheek.

"Has the truck shown up yet?" he asked after Kayla had paid the parking fee.

She shook her head. "They called a little after noon today. Ran into engine trouble this side of El Paso and managed to limp into Fort Stockton, where they were lucky enough to find the part they needed, but it still set them back more than three hours. They expect to arrive at our place around eight tonight."

"What about the security system?"

"The utility company strung the new power

line from the road to the vineyard yesterday, and the security people worked all day yesterday and today putting in the fencing and the poles for lights and cameras."

She turned onto Loop 410. "They had a problem, though, with a transponder or something, so the system isn't up yet. Hopefully by tomorrow evening."

"Tomorrow? We need security tonight. The stock I got may be better than the first batch. Not chenin blanc this time, but an exceptionally fine chardonnay. We can supplement them later from our own cuttings if we want to expand."

"I'm amazed you were able to get anything."

"I wouldn't settle for *anything*," he quietly admonished her. "You can't make good wine from inferior grapes. Go with the best or not at all."

She felt suddenly very tired. The last thing she needed now was a lecture.

He glanced over and smiled apologetically. "Sorry. I got carried away."

She gave him a weak smile and made the turn off the loop onto the road to Homestead.

"It's just that we can't afford to let someone else damage these cuttings," he said. "I was counting on the security system tonight."

"They'll be all right in the barn."

"I'm not going to take a chance. I'll stay out there tonight."

"Dad—"

He patted her shoulder. "It's just for one night, honey. Maybe I'll move the TV out there." He snickered. "If that doesn't aggravate me enough to keep me awake, nothing will."

Unlike Daryl, who'd been a TV junkie, her father hated TV even more than he disliked sloppy joes. Except for a particular news program, the History Channel and seasonal sports, he never watched it, which suited Kayla fine. That way Megan wasn't exposed to it, either. She much preferred her daughter read a book.

Forty-five minutes later they pulled up in front of the house and found Ethan leaning against the side of his truck, ankles and arms crossed, cowboy hat casting his brooding face in shadow. Kayla's heart skipped a beat at the sight of him, an image she knew would remain fixed in her mind for the rest of her life. He watched as she and Megan and her father climbed out of her car, then came to greet them.

ETHAN WELCOMED BOYD home, all the time keeping Kayla in his peripheral vision as she walked around the front of the car. He didn't miss her tension, her wariness that he might still be angry.

He was angry but not at her, not anymore. He wasn't the man she wanted him to be, or that he wanted to be, but that wasn't her fault.

"How was your trip?" he asked her father.

"Productive." Boyd was about to say more when Megan interrupted them.

"Did you feed Birdsong?" she asked Ethan.

He laughed. Her love of that horse raised his spirits. "Sure did, sprite. Mucked out her stall, too. She sends her regards."

Kayla dragged her daughter away. "Let's go inside, honey. We don't want you getting sick again. I think you can trust Ethan to take good care of his horses. You coming inside?" she asked her father.

"I want to take a look at the security system first."

"I'll go with you." Ethan pushed off the side of his truck. "I expected Kayla to call me before the installers left, so we could go over procedures with them."

"Didn't she tell you? The system isn't up yet." They headed toward the vineyard. "Won't be ready until tomorrow. They ran into technical problems of some sort. Real inconvenient. My shipment of cuttings will be arriving this evening, and after what happened I sure don't want to leave them unguarded. I told her I'd spend the night in the barn. Anybody showing up tonight will be looking down the barrel of a twelve-gauge."

"I'll spell you," Ethan said.

"No need for that, but thanks anyway."

They'd reached the newly installed fence line. Twenty-foot metal poles had been positioned every fifty feet, topped with lights and cameras. Ethan recognized laser sensors as well, though the casual observer might not notice them. An interruption in their signals would result in any of several combinations of responses.

"I don't mind," Ethan said. "As I told Kayla, the security of your place is in my own best interest. I want to catch whoever's messing with you before he messes with me."

Boyd nodded. "That's enough to keep anybody awake at night."

He examined the ground where Kayla had torn out plants and checked the tension of the heavy wires.

"You want the early shift or the late?" Ethan asked.

Boyd considered. "Since I'm still on West Coast time, why don't I take the early shift. You can relieve me at…three o'clock, all right?"

"Make it two. I'm usually up by six, anyway."

They turned toward the tin building that served as their warehouse. Inside there was an earthy smell, one that Ethan found invigorating. An old tractor sat forlornly in one corner. Cobwebs laced the rafters, but the hard-packed dirt floor was clear and unobstructed.

"When's the shipment due?" Ethan asked.

"Kayla said around eight, barring another vehicle breakdown, of course."

Returning to the house, they told Kayla about their plans for the night. She invited Ethan to stay for supper.

He hesitated. It was clear the invitation was a courtesy rather than a desire for his company. In fact, she seemed downright jittery.

He couldn't blame her, not after the way he'd treated her on Sunday. She'd made a generous offer for the sake of kids who needed love, and he'd turned it around to make her look thoughtless and incompetent.

"We're having ham and macaroni and cheese," Megan informed him gleefully. "Macaroni and cheese is one of my most favorites. You could have had sloppy joes with us if you'd come over last night. We only have them when Grandpa isn't here, 'cause he doesn't like them."

Boyd tucked his tongue in his cheek and grinned sheepishly at Kayla.

"But he likes macaroni and cheese, so we're having that tonight," his granddaughter went on.

"Do join us." This time Kayla sounded sincere.

"Okay, thanks. Then I can help you unload your shipment when it arrives," he said.

OVER THE DINNER TABLE Kayla found herself falling once again under Ethan's spell. He chatted with her father about land and agriculture and asked good questions about grapes and wine making, which impressed the older man immensely. He joked with Megan, elicited stories from her about what she was learning in school and especially about the pageant she was going to star in. Finally, he asked her opinion about the handicapped kids who'd come out to ride, endearing the child by treating her like an adult.

He even raved over Kayla's macaroni and cheese.

Since she knew he'd seen the box it came out of, she accepted the compliment as a kind of peace offering, a reassurance that they could still be friends. They'd barely cleared the table when they heard the harsh blare of an 18-wheeler's air horn.

"Time to get to work." He rose and carried his plate to the counter by the sink as if he were one of the family.

"I'll be out in a couple of minutes," she announced, "after I stack the dishwasher."

She watched him amble out the door behind her father and Megan—who should be going to bed. It amazed her how easily he fit at their table and how comfortable her father and Megan were with him. A family man without a family.

BOYD LEFT THE BARN shortly after two, and Ethan settled into the worn easy chair they'd brought from the house, opened one of the magazines on viticulture stacked on the wooden crate beside him and adjusted the gooseneck lamp, intent on studying up on an industry he knew very little about.

The first periodical was clearly intended for dedicated professionals. He didn't even recognize the vocabulary and wasn't sure he could pronounce half the words. He had no idea what xylem-feeding insects or a phylloxera-resistant rootstock were, but surmised you didn't want the first but you did want the second. He put the journal aside in favor of a glossy magazine that showed more promise.

He learned that grapevines were self-pollinators, that some could produce for more than a hundred years, though the average life-span was more like twenty-five. He was marveling that a single vine could yield enough juice for three to six bottles of wine when he thought he heard footsteps outside.

Quietly setting the magazine aside, he rose from the chair, picked up the shotgun leaning against a hay bale and tiptoed to the small portal within the much larger barn door. Regretting that he hadn't turned off the table lamp, he was nevertheless prepared to yank the door wide, when it creaked open on its own. He waited, unsure what to expect. A gun perhaps?

Kayla.

Ethan let out his breath. "What on earth are you doing here?"

She froze midmotion, one foot in, the other out. "Oh, there you are. I wondered…" She glanced to the empty chair.

He took her arm and helped her the rest of the way in. She was wearing a velvety jumpsuit.

"Kayla, it's almost three o'clock in the morning." He closed the door behind her, his mind racing. "What are you doing up…out here?" Relief softened the harshness of his words.

"I couldn't sleep and thought you might like company." She lifted the thermos in her left hand but held on to the quilt draped over her right arm. "It's getting chilly out. Figured you might be cold in this big unheated barn."

Cold? The sight of her had warmth spreading through him. Besides, the night was unusually mild. He'd been tempted to open the big door, but there wasn't a breeze stirring, and he didn't want the exposure.

Here they were, alone in a barn in the middle of the night. He shouldn't be entertaining thoughts of kissing her again, but he couldn't seem to help himself.

"Coffee," he said inanely. "Thanks."

He motioned her to the chair, content to take

a prickly hay bale for himself, but she waved the invitation away. Spreading the quilt on the hay, she patted a place beside her for him.

It was late. His mind was fogged by fatigue and longing. She was driving him crazy.

"You want..." He held up the thermos.

"Sure, if you'll join me."

He tossed the stale remnants of his mug outside, refilled it and poured hers into the thermos cap.

"I appreciate the coffee—" he nodded to the quilt they were sitting on "—and the creature comforts." He sipped his steaming drink. "But what really brought you out here, Kayla?"

She held her cup in both hands and stared into it. "We need to talk." She spoke in little more than a whisper. "I want to apologize for the other day."

"What for? I'm the one who should be apologizing for my bad manners."

She looked at him strangely. "I offended you. I didn't mean to."

"I overreacted. It wasn't your fault."

"I'm worried about the children."

"I know you are. So am I."

He set their mugs on the small table within arm's reach and clasped both her hands in his.

"I care very deeply about you, Kayla, more than I ever thought I could care for another person. If I were the marrying kind, you are the only woman I'd want to spend the rest of my life with."

He leaned forward and gently kissed her on the lips, held it a few too-brief seconds.

"But I'm not the marrying kind. You know why. That's not going to change, Kayla. I'm sorry."

Her eyes were staring into his, searching. He wished so much that she could find in him what she wanted, that he could offer her what she deserved.

Climbing to her feet, she placed her hands on his shoulders. This time she initiated a kiss of her own, a kiss that was gentle but insistent.

His breath caught. He couldn't help responding. Climbing to his feet, their lips still locked, he pulled her against him. He swept his hand over her back and up through her silky hair to cup the back of her head.

Finally he forced himself to pull away.

"I think you'd better go back to the house now," he said in a strained, husky voice.

She let several heartbeats go by. "Is that what you really want, Ethan?"

He closed his eyes, praying the ache for her would go away, knowing it wouldn't. "No."

"Neither do I." She gazed up at him sadly. "But I suppose you're right." She dropped her arms from around his neck and moved slowly toward the exit.

"Good night, Kayla," he said from behind her.

Without turning she said, "Good night, Ethan," and stepped through the door.

CHAPTER THIRTEEN

KAYLA WAS TYING UP new vines along the second row of the vineyard Wednesday afternoon, trying very hard not to think about the night before when her cell phone went off. The school nurse was calling.

"Mrs. Price, I'm concerned about Megan. She's still having trouble breathing. I've supervised her use of the inhaler, but I think you ought to come and get her."

"I'll be right there."

Kayla turned off the phone and hurried over to her father who was working several rows away and explained the call.

He straightened stiffly. "Do you want me to go with you?"

"No, I can handle it."

The twenty-minute drive took fifteen. She found Megan in the school nurse's office, the nurse sitting next to her, holding her hand. Megan's breathing was arduous, her skin pale and slightly sweaty.

The woman looked up, clearly worried. "I wasn't sure if I should call you or 911."

"I'll take her home and put her on the nebulizer. She responds better to that. Maybe it's something around here that's irritating her."

"I don't know what. We don't have any oleander on the school grounds anymore. I even had them cut down all the cedars that were up against the building," the nurse said, "but of course the pollen is still in the air."

"There's no telling at this point," Kayla commented as she drew her wheezing daughter to her feet, stroked her arms sympathetically and led her to the door.

"Megan tells me Heather Gibbs and Brad Estes take the school bus to your place on Wednesdays," the nurse said, following along. "If you don't want them there today I can have them take their regular bus."

Kayla considered a moment. She hated to disappoint the two children. "They can still come over. If Megan isn't better I'll have my father drive them home."

The nurse walked with them down the corridor toward the exit to the parking lot. "I've heard so many good things about the riding program you've started. What you're doing is really wonderful. Their teachers tell me they've seen a marked improvement in Brad's and Heather's attitudes and school performance."

It was nice to hear. Kayla had noticed a change in the two. She only hoped the other children would benefit, as well.

By the time Heather and Brad showed up at Stony Hill an hour and a half later, Megan was much improved, but Kayla wasn't about to let her go over to Ethan's place.

"But I miss Birdsong," the girl complained.

"Birdsong wouldn't want you to be sick," Kayla told her. "Let's wait until you can really enjoy being with her."

Boyd agreed to drive the other two and then take them home. Kayla gave him the address and directions.

Ten minutes after they left, the phone rang.

"Your dad says Megan's sick." Ethan sounded as concerned as she felt. He really cared. This wasn't just a polite inquiry. "Is she going to be all right?"

He hadn't stayed for breakfast that morning. When Boyd had gone out to the barn to invite him in, he'd excused himself, saying he had horses to feed.

She'd greeted the news with a mixture of disappointment and relief. It was becoming increasingly difficult to hide the way she felt in his presence.

"Springtime is always a challenge. I just have to keep her indoors for a few days. Respiratory problems aren't fun."

"Scary, if you ask me. But you're sure she'll be okay?"

"We've been through this, Ethan. She'll be fine."

"Call me if you need anything, anything at all."

"I will. Thanks." She hung up feeling better, knowing he was close and willing to help.

By the following morning Megan seemed fully recovered, and Kayla let her go to school, this time with the admonition not to go outside during recess or at lunchtime, but to stay inside where the air-conditioning provided at least some filtration.

But that afternoon she received another call from the nurse. Megan was having trouble breathing again. This was the part Daryl always resented—having to drop whatever he was doing when his daughter needed him, as if she had any choice.

Once more the nebulizer brought relief and by Friday morning Megan was again back to her old self, but Kayla decided to keep her home, anyway.

"M-o-m, we have to practice today," Megan whined. "Mrs. Franklin will give my part to someone else if I'm not there."

Kayla knew how much her daughter wanted to be in the pageant, and that she was a handful at home when she was feeling well, but Kayla couldn't take any chances. The episodes were getting worse, and it seemed obvious there was something in the environment at school that was triggering them.

"I'll talk to her," she promised. "I'm sure Mrs. Franklin will let you keep the part."

"Not if I'm not there!" the girl shouted.

"Megan, please calm down. You know this isn't good for you."

"I hate being sick. I don't want to be sick anymore."

Kayla's heart ached. "I know you don't, honey. I wish you weren't, too, but it isn't your fault. It's not anyone's fault. What we have to do is make sure you stay well, and for today, that means staying at home and staying in the house."

"You're mean!" the girl yelled, ran to her room and slammed the door.

Under other circumstances Kayla would

have been all over her for her bad behavior, but jumping on her right now would only exacerbate the problem. She'd give her a few minutes to calm down.

At lunchtime, Kayla was able to reach Mrs. Franklin. The teacher was sympathetic and very complimentary about Megan's performance in her classroom.

"She's bright, obedient and inquisitive. Keeps me on my toes, I can tell you," she said with a laugh. "You can assure her she'll still be the star of the pageant."

Kayla was relieved at the news. "Is there anything Megan can do to keep up with the work she's missing?"

"I told them yesterday to take their workbooks home. If she has hers, she can do the next exercise or two. Otherwise don't worry about it. She's quick. She'll pick up what she missed."

After lunch—grilled cheese and tomato soup, another one of Megan's favorites—encouraged by Mrs. Franklin's promise of the leading role, Megan went to her room, opened her book bag and set to work on her assignment.

The excitement of the morning had finally taken its toll, though. When Kayla looked in on her a few minutes later, Megan was having trouble breathing again, and Kayla put her on the nebulizer. That seemed to help for a little while, but not nearly as long as it usually did. By the time the school bus dropped Heather and Brad off, Megan's breathing was dangerously labored.

"MEGAN HAVING ANOTHER attack?" Ethan asked when he saw Kayla's father get out of the Toyota with Heather and Brad.

The worry in Boyd's nod made Ethan wonder just how bad it was this time.

"Do you want me to take the kids home after their lesson?" Ethan asked. "Glad to, if it'll help."

Boyd shook off the suggestion. "Thanks, but you're busy, too."

The farrier had arrived half an hour ago and was shoeing horses as Ethan and Carter brought them in from the pastures.

"Besides," Boyd added, "there really isn't anything I can do that Kayla isn't. If she needs me, she'll call."

Ethan was tempted to phone Kayla, but Boyd was right. There was nothing he could do and he didn't want to make a nuisance of himself.

The kids saddled their mounts and led them out of the barn to the riding arena. Their confidence and enthusiasm had grown over the past two months. Ethan smiled at the rapt expressions on the youngsters' faces as they walked their horses to the corral gate.

He checked and tightened cinches, adjusted a neck strap and gave each child a leg up into the saddle. The lesson began with walking, then progressed to a trot.

"When can I lope?" Brad asked.

"Think you're ready today?"

"Yes!" Brad held up a fist in triumph.

"This first time, I want you to hold on to the reins with your right hand, as usual, and the horn with your left."

"I don't have to—"

"Hold it with your left," Ethan insisted, "till you get used to the rhythm of the horse. I'll tell you when to let go."

Even at nine the male instinct to bull his way through a situation was strong. Ethan wasn't surprised by the initial look of terror on the boy's face when the big horse broke into a controlled gallop. In truth, Joker wasn't moving much faster than at an extended trot, but the impression for the inexperienced was of much greater speed and a lack of control. To Brad's credit, he didn't panic, though he hung on to the saddle horn. It took him a second or two to register Ethan's command to sit deeper in the saddle. Once he did, the rocking-horse rhythm took over and a smile spread across the boy's face.

Ethan looked over at Heather. "Would you like to try?"

"Y-Yes. I guess so." She was scared.

"You don't have to if you don't think you're ready."

"Maybe I'll wait for Megan, so she can show me."

Ethan suppressed a smile. Waiting for her friend was an excuse, but Heather often looked to Megan for leadership. To her, Brad was different. He was older, and he was, after all, a boy.

Forty-five minutes later, Carter was leading the last of the geldings back to the pasture and the farrier was cooling his small gas-fired forge when Boyd waved goodbye and drove off with the children to take them home.

Ethan retreated to the house and dialed Kayla's number. The answering machine picked up. Maybe she was just busy or outside. Or the phone was turned off so Megan could sleep. Or she had the TV on too loud. He went back to his chores but returned a little while later and dialed again. This time Boyd answered.

"I called a few minutes ago, but—"

"I just walked in." Boyd sounded winded. "They're not here."

"What do you mean, not there?"

"Kayla left a note. She had to take Megan to the clinic."

"Give me a minute to clean up, and I'll pick you up in ten. We'll go into town together." Ethan hung up, only then realizing his hand was shaking.

KAYLA KEPT BITING HER LIP. Her hands were squeezing the steering wheel so hard, her fingers hurt.

"We're almost there," she said, trying desperately to sound calm and assuring.

Megan, strapped into the seat beside her, was making horrible sucking sounds as she inhaled. Her daughter was struggling for breath, and all Kayla could do was sit there and keep her foot from stomping the gas pedal to the floor. She was already driving over the speed limit. Fortunately this stretch of road was long and straight.

She'd checked out the small clinic in town when they'd first arrived, knowing eventually she'd have to go there for something.

Her mind raced, trying to sort through the information she'd received on that brief visit. A physician's assistant, not a doctor, ran the place. What was her name? Kristin something. She wanted to say Gallagher, but that was the senator's name, so that couldn't be right. There was a doctor…Louise Hernandez…who came on Wednesdays from San Antonio. Today was Friday, which meant she wouldn't be there. The P.A. had been very nice and seemed quite competent, but this wasn't a broken arm or sprained knee. Asthma was life threatening. There wasn't much time to evaluate, just act.

Kayla wasn't doing herself any good focusing on the negative as she zipped into town, but it was hard to think positive when her child, the most precious thing in the world to her, was fighting for every breath.

She rolled into Homestead on Bluebonnet Street. The town square with its ornate old courthouse was on her left. On her right, a few cars were parked diagonally in front of the beauty salon and the saddle shop. She drove past the newspaper office. Pickups filled the spaces in front of the post office and hardware store. At Main, she swung sharply left and pulled into an empty spot in front of the clinic. Megan's pale skin was turning blue around the mouth.

"We're there, honey. It'll just be a minute now."

Kayla jumped out of the Toyota and called out, "I need help!" She ran around the hood of the car. Yanking open the passenger door, she unbuckled Megan and was trying to scoop her up when someone touched her back, making her involuntarily flinch. Turning her head, she saw a bald man in a white smock. He motioned her aside, bent and picked the child up as if she was no heavier than a tea bag and set her gently in the wheelchair he'd brought out.

"What's the problem?" asked the small middle-aged woman who was holding the front door as he maneuvered up the ramp.

"Severe asthma attack," Kayla explained.

"Any idea what brought it on?"

"She's been having problems for the past week, but until now her inhaler and nebulizer kept it under control. I figured it was just spring pollen."

"Could be," the woman said as they moved quickly into an examining room. She was wearing a green smock over loose chinos. Kayla looked at her embroidered name but couldn't decipher it.

The woman caught her eye. "Call me Ski. It's a lot easier to pronounce than Mszeslowski, even for me. I'm a P.A. That's Max Zimmerman. He's a nurse," she added, nodding to the big man with a shaved head and several tattoos on his brawny arms.

Max lifted Megan onto the examining table with ease. Megan's breathing was agonizingly painful.

Ski listened to Megan's heart and lungs through her stethoscope while the nurse put a blood pressure cuff on her arm. "How long has she been this way?"

"I gave her a nebulizer treatment about two hours ago. She seemed to improve. She was tired but alert. Then about half an hour ago she became very lethargic. I was afraid she'd stopped breathing altogether, so I used the epi-pen, but it didn't seem to do much good. I got her here as fast as I could. I would have—"

"BP 110 over 65," Max announced.

The woman stuck a digital thermometer in Megan's ear. Kayla wasn't sure, but she thought it read 97.8. Or maybe it was 98.7. Didn't matter. Either way, she wasn't running a fever. One less thing to worry about.

The nurse affixed another cuff to Megan's left arm and plugged the lead into a machine he'd pulled over. Readings appeared instantly.

Ski patted Kayla's hand. "You did the right thing. Don't worry. We're going to take good care of her. Are you aware of any allergies she has to medications?"

"No," Kayla responded, staring as her child worked so hard to breath. *Why don't you hurry up?* She wanted to scream.

"Max, I'll draw blood so we can check blood gasses, while you prepare the nebulizer. Then I'll give her a shot of Solu-Medrol."

Kayla stood by as the two worked with smooth efficiency in the close confines of the small examining room, each keeping out of the other's way. Ski inserted a needle in the vein of Megan's wrist. The girl didn't even flinch, maybe because it was done so expertly, but it was equally likely that Megan simply didn't have the energy to respond. Every ounce of her strength was being consumed by the effort to breathe.

Max moved in a positive-pressure machine and attached a bottle of abuterol to the long plastic tube leading to the face mask. Putting the vial of blood aside, Ski filled a syringe and injected Megan in the vein near her left elbow.

"This is a higher dose of epinephrine to open the airways. It should do the trick in a minute," she said.

Kayla shivered at the realization that this was

trial and error. She wanted a cure now, this minute, not experiments.

"Kayla?" She heard a man's voice from the outer room.

"Dad?"

Ski threw back the curtain. Ethan was standing beside her father. Both men looked terrified. He... They were here to support her. She wasn't alone.

"We came as soon as I found your note." Boyd stared at his granddaughter, who was barely awake.

Ethan looked at the woman attending the girl. "Where's Kristin?" he asked.

"At an in-service training conference in Houston," the P.A. answered. "I'm Ski, her relief."

He nodded toward the patient. "How is she?"

"She's never had an attack this severe." Kayla's eyes were glued to her daughter, who continued to work for each breath.

"I'm Max." The nurse gently fitted the oxygen mask over Megan's nose and mouth.

There were more mumbled introductions all around and everyone stood watching the child on the examining table.

"Is she going to be okay?" Ethan finally

asked, voicing Kayla's fear that her little girl might not be.

She didn't realize she was crying until Ethan put his arm around her. She collapsed against him. He smelled of soap, clean skin and fresh deodorant, and she realized he must have showered and changed clothes before coming here.

Kayla saw Max give the P.A. an inquiring look.

"Her breathing has eased up a little, but she's not responding as quickly as I'd hoped," Ski acknowledged calmly. "I'm going to give her a steroid shot while Max calls Dr. Hernandez. Louise may want us to bring Megan to the medical center in San Antonio, where they have more elaborate facilities."

"It'll take us at least thirty minutes to get there," Ethan said. "Closer to forty-five if we run into heavy traffic."

"Dr. Hernandez can order their medevac chopper to pick her up here. We use the parking lot in back as our helipad. Max, would you call her now, please?"

"Hurry," Kayla begged.

The burly nurse slipped out of the crowded room. Everyone stared at Megan as Kayla stood at her side, gently brushing her hair with her hand. They could hear Max talking on the phone outside in the reception area, the words indistinct, but the tone disturbing.

He stepped back into the room two minutes later, his expression not encouraging.

"What is it?" Kayla cried out.

For a moment the only sound in the room was the harsh, tortured wheezing of the semiconscious girl on the examining table.

"The helicopter isn't available," Max said. "There's been a multicar pileup on the interstate. It'll be at least an hour, maybe two, before they can get here."

"They've got to come now," Kayla nearly screamed.

Ethan gathered her in his arms.

"We can drive her there faster," Boyd declared and shifted, obviously prepared to go.

"The accident has the intersection of I-10 and Loop 1610 blocked up for miles in all directions," Max countered. "You'd have to drive at least sixty miles around it and approach the medical center from the other side. That would extend the trip to more like two hours, assuming access from the other side is open."

"What are we going to do?" Boyd asked.

Kayla collapsed into Ethan's embrace. "We have to do something. We can't just stand here. Please, please." *Don't let my little girl die.*

IMAGES FLASHED before Ethan's eyes. His sister's last breath, the sight of his mother reduced to hysteria, then retreating into impenetrable silence, only to fade away in her sleep a year later.

He couldn't bear to see Kayla lose her only child. He wasn't sure he could survive another death. There'd been so many.

"Give me two minutes." He left the room.

He'd seen Clint Gallagher's helicopter flying the perimeter of his ranch when he and Boyd were pulling away from Stony Hill. If there was anyone he hated, it was the owner of the Four Aces Ranch. The state senator who'd used his power to destroy the KC Enterprises consortium and ultimately drive his father to suicide. But personal enmity meant nothing now. Ethan would kiss Gallagher's feet rather than see Megan die.

Last fall Ethan had trained a wild mustang for Ramiro Sanchez, a ranch hand on the Four Aces, a task the old caballero had considered impossible. Taking a chance that Sanchez could help, he punched in the number he still had in his cell phone directory.

Sanchez answered on the first ring. "Yo."

"Ramiro, this is Ethan Ritter."

"Eh, *mi amigo*—"

Ethan cut him off and explained the situation, that there was a girl at the clinic in Homestead who would die—actually saying the word scared him to death—unless she was transported to San Antonio immediately, but that the medevac helicopter was tied up.

"I saw the senator's chopper flying a few minutes ago. I need to ask him...beg him to come and get her and fly her down to the hospital in San Antonio."

Sanchez didn't hesitate. "Hang on. I'm putting you on hold, but don't hang up." The line clicked and went silent.

Ethan's stomach burned. His legs felt weak. Sweat rolled down the back of his neck, beaded his forehead and stung his eyes. He tried to rub it away but to no avail. His hands, too, were wet.

The next sound in his ear was loud, disorienting. A whop-whop thudding in a droning background of static. Then he heard a voice.

"Ritter, what the blazes is going on?" The great man himself. Sanchez had patched him through to the chopper.

"Senator, there's a little girl here in the Homestead clinic who's going to die unless she gets to the San Antonio Medical Center immediately. The medevac chopper's tied up because of a pileup on the interstate, and the crash site has road access from here completely blocked. Your helicopter is her only hope."

There was a pause, and then he heard a different voice. "Ethan, this is Travis." Gallagher's youngest son. "Where can we land?"

Ethan felt as if a huge weight had been lifted off his chest. "The parking lot behind the clinic."

The old man came on again, barking out orders. "Make sure it's clear, Ritter. Push cars out of the way. Do whatever you have to so we can get in and get out. We'll be there in three minutes."

"Yes, sir. Thank you, sir."

He heard Gallagher giving his son directions before the connection went dead.

Galvanized, despite the painful lump in his throat, Ethan ran back to the others. "Get Megan ready to transfer right away. Gallagher's chopper will be here in three minutes." He saw the astonishment in everyone's faces. He turned to Boyd.

"We need to clear the parking lot behind us. I'll push them out of the way with my truck if I have to."

"My car's back there." Max dug into his

pants pocket, pulled out a key ring and tossed it to Ethan, who caught it one-handed.

"Mine, too," Ski said. "Keys are in my purse in the bottom right-hand drawer under the counter in the reception area."

"You move hers," Ethan told Boyd. "I'll move Max's."

"I need to go with Megan," Kayla insisted.

"I don't know if there'll be room. It's not a real big chopper," Ethan told her. "If he can only take one passenger, I think it should be Ski." He looked at the P.A.

She nodded. "Max, get a portable oxygen bottle. We'll put her on that for the trip. Also, I'll take an intubation kit just in case."

"It's going to be okay, baby." Tears were streaming down Kayla's face as she stroked Megan's forehead. "You're going to be okay."

Megan, straining for each breath, was exhausted by the effort. Her eyes were open and staring.

As Ski packed an emergency bag and Max changed the air supply from the machine to a small oxygen bottle, which he strapped between her legs, Boyd and Ethan moved the vehicles. Ethan hadn't even turned off the engine of Max's car when he heard the beat of helicopter blades.

The parking lot was paved but dusty, a fact that became patently evident the moment the whirlybird began its descent. Shielding his eyes from the blast of flying dirt, Ethan approached the aircraft as the door on the right swung open.

"Where is she?" Gallagher growled.

The back door of the clinic opened and the gurney rolled toward them.

"Thank you for doing this, Senator," Ethan said.

"I can take one person with her. Who's going?"

"The P.A."

Kayla stood at the edge of the pavement gripping her father's arm as Ethan and the nurse lifted the nearly unconscious child into the cabin of the chopper. Ski scrambled in behind her.

A second later, the door closed and the whine of the engine rose to a high-pitched scream. The helicopter lifted off.

Kayla's tearstained face was filthy from the dirt kicked up in the rotor wash. Looking as if he'd been poleaxed, Boyd clung to his daughter. It would be hard to say who was consoling whom.

"I need to be with her," Kayla moaned.

Ethan raced to the back door. "We'll take my truck."

WASHING HER FACE and hands helped, but only marginally. Kayla's stomach ached. Her head throbbed. Her chest felt as if a vise were squeezing it. As determined as she was to go to San Antonio, she wasn't sure her legs would carry her out of the restroom. Inhaling deeply, she straightened and joined the others in the waiting room of the small country clinic.

"Brewed a fresh pot of coffee." Max handed Ethan a thermos, probably his own. He offered Boyd a paper sack. "You've got cups, cream and sugar packets, stirrers and napkins in here."

"Thank you," the older man said, his voice a bit wobbly.

Max turned to Kayla. "Megan's in good hands. Ski's the best. Your daughter will be fine."

Kayla gave him a hug. "Thanks for your help."

"Let's move," Ethan urged.

The image of Megan as she was being lifted into the chopper crowded Kayla's mind. Turning abruptly, she crossed to the door her father was holding open and strode outside.

Ethan had pulled up in front of the building, taking up two parking spaces, not that it made any difference. There was no one around. Homestead didn't have a traffic light, much less a traffic jam. What few businesses were still operating around the town square had closed half an hour ago, and the people in them departed for the day.

Ethan climbed behind the wheel of the three-quarter-ton pickup with Boyd sitting shotgun beside him. Kayla crawled into the backseat of the crew cab.

Switching on the radio, Ethan flipped through stations trying to find traffic news. They learned that there had been a sixteen-vehicle pileup involving a tank truck carrying hazardous chemicals. A large area around the cloverleaf intersection had already been evacuated and all traffic was being diverted. At least seven people had been killed and as many as thirty injured. The cause of the mishap was under investigation but was believed to be the result of a speeder cutting off the 18-wheeler. Casualties were being flown by helicopter to several hospitals in the San Antonio area.

Since Homestead was thirty miles outside the sprawling South Texas city, Ethan had more road options than if they were closer in, but those additional choices also added extra miles.

"I'll have to take a very long way around," he told his passengers. "Let's hope other drivers aren't using the same secondary roads."

"How long will it take us?" Kayla remembered making the trip in less than forty-five minutes. The medical complex, she knew, was on the outskirts of the city.

"An hour and a half minimum, assuming there are no holdups along the way."

She groaned. It sounded like forever.

Ethan flipped on his high beams. "Any idea what caused this attack?" he asked a minute later.

"I think I may know," Boyd said.

CHAPTER FOURTEEN

"I DON'T HAVE ASTHMA," Boyd explained to Ethan, "but my eyes have been itching like crazy lately. I asked the pharmacist when I was picking up my arthritis prescription the other day if he had any idea what could be causing it. I knew it wasn't the medication, since I've been taking it for years."

Kayla wished he'd get to the point.

"He said it might be pecan tassels."

"Pecan tassels?" she asked, clearly bewildered.

"Pecan trees are in bloom right now," Ethan explained. "Their blossoms are green tassels. You probably haven't noticed them, but some people are highly allergic."

He turned to Boyd. "I reckon you don't have pecan trees in Oregon."

"Nope, and I've never had this kind of allergic reaction before, either. I noticed when I was taking the kids home the other day that their school is surrounded by pecan trees."

"That could explain why she was having such a hard time at school," Kayla said. "But what about at home? We have a couple of pecan trees on our place, and she doesn't seem to have a problem there."

"Except today. Ours only started tasseling yesterday," her father said.

Ethan nodded. "Probably a different variety. Later blooming." He turned onto a farm-to-market road that wasn't as wide as the ones they'd been traveling but was in good condition. It was also practically empty. Ethan pressed on the accelerator and leveled off ten miles above the speed limit. "I sure hope my deer whistle works," he mumbled.

"And I hope that security system we installed works as advertised," Boyd added.

Darkness had fallen by the time they reached the medical center. It felt like midnight. The parking lot was packed, so Ethan dropped Kayla and her father off at the emergency entrance. Ten minutes later he entered the massive, brightly lit building. They were nowhere in sight. After a quick inquiry at the desk, however, he rode the elevator to the third floor.

He found Kayla and her father pacing a small alcove just beyond the nurses' station. "What's the news?" he asked.

"We're waiting for the doctor now," Boyd said.

"Why won't they tell me anything?" Kayla cried.

Her semblance of calm was gone. She twisted her hands and bit her lips, on the verge of tears. Ethan instinctively wrapped his arms around her. She accepted the embrace hungrily, then backed off, as if she didn't want to be comforted.

A woman in a white coat marched down the corridor, slowing only when she got within a few yards of them. She introduced herself as Dr. Louise Hernandez. "Let's sit down." She motioned them to the chairs against the wall.

Small and delicate, the physician pulled up one of the molded plastic chairs and sat directly in front of Kayla. She took her hand.

"Your daughter has been stabilized," she said. "Getting her here so quickly undoubtedly saved her life, but we had to intubate her. She's being treated now with respiratory medication as well as epinephrine and cordicosteroids to reduce the swelling in her airways and lungs."

"But she's going to be all right," Kayla half stated, half asked.

"She's in intensive care and being monitored very closely. I'm concerned that she may be developing pneumonia."

"Pneumonia!" Kayla gasped. "But—"

"We're doing everything we can to prevent that, but it could be several hours before we know for sure."

"She will recover," Boyd insisted.

"We're doing everything we can."

In other words, we don't know.

Kayla covered her face with her hands and let out a ragged sob. Sitting beside her, Ethan put an arm around her, pressing her head to his shoulder.

"Shh. She'll come through," he said soothingly, and prayed he was right. "She's tough."

Kayla finally lifted her head, revealing raw, bloodshot eyes. "Can I see her?"

The doctor nodded. "I must warn you. She has a tube down her throat and there are machines monitoring her. I don't want you to be shocked by what you see. Just remember we're doing everything possible, and in spite of appearances, her chances are very good."

"I just want to be with her," Kayla said.

"Of course. She's sleeping now, partly from the medication we've given her but also from exhaustion. She might still be able to hear you, though, so speak quietly to her, let her know you're there and give her plenty of encouragement. That's often the best medicine."

Only one person at a time was allowed in the room. Ethan and Boyd stood outside and watched through a large window as Kayla took her daughter's right hand and talked to her. They didn't need to hear her to know Kayla was being upbeat. To see Kayla's face was to know that beneath each syllable her heart was breaking.

So was Ethan's.

"You saved her life," Boyd said.

Ethan didn't respond.

"Kayla told me about your relationship with Gallagher, yet you called him for help."

"Wouldn't you have?" Ethan asked.

"For my granddaughter? I'd call on the devil himself. But she's not your kin."

"Little girls don't deserve to have bad things happen to them," he muttered.

He loved Kayla, too, as he'd never loved any other woman. He'd given up having children of his own, but for the first time in his life he was seriously regretting his vow never to marry.

"Thank you," Boyd said, his voice choked.

Ethan found himself embraced by the older man. Self-consciously they broke apart a minute later and continued to watch the scene inside intensive care.

Ten minutes passed. The doctor went in and

tapped Kayla on the arm and invited her to step out. Kayla hesitated, but didn't resist as she was led from the room.

"Doctor," Ethan asked, when they were all together in the hallway again, "can you tell me what happened to Ski, the P.A. who came with Megan in the helicopter?"

"She went back on the chopper. I heard it was Senator Gallagher's, that he flew them down here. Is that true?"

"Yes," Ethan confirmed with a nod.

"Well, he saved Megan's life."

"We'll always be grateful to him," Ethan said.

EVEN IN HER DISTRAUGHT state, the irony of the situation wasn't lost on Kayla. Ethan had turned to the person he despised most for help, and now that person would be credited with saving Megan's life. Not that she wasn't indebted to Gallagher. The state senator certainly deserved praise for acting quickly and unconditionally, but to Kayla the real credit would always belong to Ethan.

Perhaps she was being cynical, but it seemed to her Gallagher had had little choice in the matter. Rejecting such a plea would have been suicide for a politician. Ethan, on the other hand, had had to look beyond himself, beyond his hatred for the man. Then he'd had to swallow his pride and ask for help. That couldn't have been easy, but he'd done it without hesitation.

The hours dragged by.

Kayla was allowed to visit Megan for a few minutes every hour, as was Boyd. Kayla wondered what the visits were costing her father, who managed to put on a positive face, but his eyes told a different story.

Kayla didn't remember her mother, who'd been killed in a car crash when Kayla was two. She had no recollection of her six-year-old brother who'd been in the same accident, either. Jimmy had lingered on for several days before finally succumbing, as well. She learned later that her dad had sat by his hospital bed the entire time, never leaving, always hopeful that the boy would recover. This vigil must be torture for him, stirring up old memories.

He'd been a good dad to her. There had been times when she wished he'd been more affectionate, but she'd never doubted that he loved her. She told him that she loved him from time to time, but she didn't gush. That kind of emotionalism would have embarrassed him. For him, saying it seemed to be enough, so she respected the boundaries he set.

The ICU nurse let Ethan in to see Megan once, too, and again Kayla wondered what seeing an eight-year-old in a hospital bed was doing to him.

He'd gone to Megan's bedside smiling and chatty about Birdsong, about the pageant she was going to star in, about how her friend Heather was waiting for her so she could start loping. He'd come out smiling, confident, he asserted, that Megan was going to be just fine.

She loved him all the more for his bravery.

She sat down beside him in the waiting area, rested her head against his shoulder and woke up an hour later with a stiff neck. As he had that day on the Broken Spoke, he gently massaged the tight muscles with his strong hands. It felt so right as she turned into the pressure of his masterful fingers and warm caress.

At 6:00 a.m. Megan rallied, and the doctor removed the tube from her throat.

"The steroids and antibiotics did the trick," Dr. Hernandez said, as if she'd known all along that everything was going to be all right. "We'll continue to monitor her for a few more hours, but I think it's safe to say the crisis has passed."

They went in to see the patient. "We can release you in a few hours, young lady," the doctor said.

"Does that mean I can go home?" Megan asked, her voice raspy. "I don't like being here."

Kayla smiled. "Yes, honey, we'll be going home soon."

"I'll give you a prescription for steroids that she can continue to take orally," the physician told Kayla. "If you notice any deterioration in her condition, contact the Homestead clinic at once. Kristin will be back from her training course on Monday."

"How long will she have to take the steroids?" Kayla asked, concerned about their long-term effect on her daughter.

"A few weeks is all. We want to make sure she doesn't have a relapse. If your suspicion is correct, that pecan pollen is the problem, that ought to be enough. By then the blooming season will be over. Don't assume, though, that that's the culprit or the sole cause. It could be a combination of things that don't pose serious problems in themselves. I know you do it anyway, but try to see what's different that could have triggered this crisis."

"Thank you, Doctor."

At noon Megan was discharged from the hospital. The four of them climbed into Ethan's truck for the drive home, a journey that took less than half as long as the night before. The highway had been cleared. In fact, there was no indication at the junction of the two major highways that anything had even happened.

MEGAN SNOOZED ON the ride back to Homestead, and so did the rest of Ethan's passengers. As he moved along with the flow of traffic, his thoughts kept returning to Kayla's proposal—that they get married to adopt Heather and Brad. A marriage of convenience.

He'd rejected her. But that was before Megan had come close to death, and he'd been reminded once more how sacred life was.

Now he was having second thoughts, not just as a way of rescuing the two foster children, but for more selfish reasons. He felt as close to Kayla and Megan as he'd ever felt to anyone. He also recognized he didn't want a false relationship, a mere business arrangement. He'd been honest when he told her he couldn't play house and then just walk away, as if they were props in a game. What he hadn't been as candid about was that he couldn't endure a facade of intimacy without going mad.

Now he knew that wouldn't be necessary. He'd never felt for any woman what he felt for

Kayla, but she'd asked for a marriage of convenience. Did that mean she wasn't interested in a true marriage with him, a permanent partnership?

Would she be willing to marry a man who couldn't give her more children? It didn't seem fair to her, yet, he decided, maybe he ought to give her the chance to tell him.

He considered making a proposal of his own, but in a pickup with her father and daughter present didn't seem like the appropriate place or time.

"I'm hungry," Megan announced from the backseat as he turned onto Bluebonnet Street.

He laughed. "I guess that means you're better." Kayla and her father both stretched.

"Ethan, if you'll drop me at the clinic, I'll pick up my car," Kayla said. "I can also thank Ski and Max for everything they did. I think there's still time for me to have Megan's prescription filled at the drugstore." Dr. Hernandez had given her enough medication to get them through the weekend.

"Okay, but here's another suggestion. I'll drop you and Megan off while Grandpa and I go to the DQ and pick up a sack of burgers."

"Good idea," Boyd said. "My treat."

"Can I have a cheeseburger with French fries?" Megan pleaded.

"And onion rings?" Kayla chimed in.

"Seems like everybody's hungry." Ethan caught Kayla's eye in the rearview mirror. "Meet you at the house?"

She nodded. "In about half an hour."

He dropped them off in front of the clinic, waved goodbye and pulled away, missing them already but also feeling strangely happy. Early Saturday afternoon, the Dairy Queen was crowded. Kayla and Megan were already home by the time he and Boyd rolled up the driveway.

Megan was definitely her old self, chattering on the phone while her mother distributed napkins and paper plates.

"Can I ride Birdsong today?" Megan asked after her first greedy bite of food. "I missed my lessons on Wednesday and Friday."

"Not today, honey. Let's make sure you're completely well before we expose you to horses."

Megan didn't seem surprised by the answer, though she gave Ethan a pleading look that begged him to run interference for her. When he didn't, she shrugged and took another bite of her cheeseburger.

After they finished, Kayla retrieved the

brown plastic pill bottle from the kitchen counter and fought with the childproof cap.

"Dr. Hernandez said for you to take your pills right after eating." She held out a tablet in the palm of her hand. "You can take this with the rest of your milk."

Megan frowned. "Is it yucky?"

"It's just a regular white pill, honey. I bet you won't even taste it."

Turning up her nose, Megan placed it on her tongue and drank her milk. She was making a gagging sound that no one believed was real when they heard a vehicle pull up in front of the house.

While Kayla tried to convince Megan she needed to go to her room with one of her favorite books and take a nap, Ethan cleared the table of greasy paper plates and napkins, and Boyd answered the doorbell.

A man's deep voice drew Ethan to the living room, where Kayla and Megan joined him a few seconds later. Sheriff Montgomery tipped his hat to Kayla.

"Glad to see you're back, young lady," he said to Megan. "Heard you got to ride in Senator Gallagher's helicopter last night."

"It was cool," she said. "He was real nice,

too. He told me I could go flying with him again if I want to."

That was news to Kayla. Megan hadn't mentioned a thing about the flight. Kayla had assumed it was because she didn't remember it or hadn't paid any attention.

"What brings you out here, Sheriff?" she asked. "Have you found whoever poisoned my vineyard?"

"Afraid not, but we're still working on it. I was wondering if you folks might have seen Brad Estes or know where he could be."

"What are you talking about?"

"He's disappeared, gone missing."

Megan's eyes grew wide and she moved to her mother and hugged her waist.

"When did this happen?" Ethan asked.

"Leona Rayborn called my office this morning around nine, said she'd just checked the boy's room but he wasn't there, and the other kids didn't know where he was. She searched the house and called the neighbors but nobody's seen him."

"Why would he run away?" Kayla asked. Had he found out the Rayborns would be leaving Homestead?

"Seems the boy got a call yesterday from his daddy—"

"I thought his father was in prison."

"Got released last week," Wade said. "Called the boy, told him he and the kid's mom had gotten together again and that they were coming to take him home."

"Oh, no," Kayla exclaimed, for the moment forgetting her daughter was clinging on to her. "Is it true?"

"We're checking now."

"How did he know where Brad was?" Ethan asked.

"Best we can figure, he called Child Protective Services, told whoever answered he was the boy's father and had just returned from a military assignment overseas and had lost the boy's current address."

"And they gave it to him?" Boyd asked, outraged.

"Shouldn't have," Wade agreed, "but apparently they did."

"When exactly did Brad disappear?" Kayla asked. "Do they know how long he's been gone?"

"Leona's sure it was after midnight, says it couldn't have been before eleven, because that's when she went to bed, after watching the first hour of the *Tonight Show*. Insists she looked into Brad's bedroom just before she turned in, like she always does, and he was asleep in his bunk bed. He has the lower one on account of his foot, so she was able to see him plainly, but when she went in to call him this morning he wasn't there."

"What time was that?" Ethan asked.

"Around eight. She lets them sleep in on Saturdays, since there's no school."

"How did he get out?"

"Looks like he climbed out the bedroom window. She found the screen loose."

"And none of the other children saw or heard him leaving?" Kayla asked skeptically.

"Kids can sleep pretty sound."

Kayla nodded, knowing how deeply Megan slept, especially when she was very tired.

"No idea where he might have gone?" Boyd asked.

"We've checked the usual places, his friends, the school, the church, but no one's seen him. I thought maybe he came over here or went to the Broken Spoke to hide out. I stopped off and talked to Carter and Luella, but neither of them have seen him. I've issued an Amber alert, and my deputies are checking the closest truck stops, just in case he tried to hitch a ride someplace."

The very thought was scary. An undersize nine-year-old boy with one foot, out on his own.

"Where would he go?" Kayla asked.

Megan looked up at her mother. "He told me once about his aunt who lives in Austin."

"Do you know the aunt's name?" the sheriff asked.

"Aunt Betty."

"Did he mention her last name or where in Austin she lives?"

"Uh-uh. Only that she lives in a real big house, and they have nurses there."

"A nursing home," Kayla muttered.

Not a very promising lead. "I'll have my people check it out. If you think of anything else that might help us find him, Megan, will you tell your mom so she can call me? Anything at all."

She nodded.

"My guess is he's headed for the Broken Spoke," Ethan said.

"Seems a reasonable assumption," Montgomery agreed. "Thing is, he's about seven miles away by road, and he'd be easily enough spotted and picked up by anyone looking for him."

"Unless he cuts cross-country," Ethan countered.

Wade considered the idea. "It's still a couple of miles, but—"

"About three miles as the crow flies," Ethan said. "There are a lot of obstacles between here and there, and plenty of places to hide."

"No way he can walk that far," Kayla pointed out. "Not on that plastic foot. He does all right over short distances, but after a while he starts limping pretty badly."

"As hot as it is today," Ethan added, "he could get into real trouble if he's out in the sun. Do we know if he's wearing a hat or carrying water?"

The sheriff shook his head. "Probably neither. Best Leona can tell, he just put yesterday's T-shirt and jeans back on and crawled out the window."

Ethan muttered something unintelligible under his breath. "He doesn't know the land, and there are all sorts of hazards out there, rocks and cactus, not to mention rattlesnakes, scorpions and fire ants." He paced. "How about calling Gallagher and asking to borrow his helicopter to help in the search? You'd be able to cover the territory a lot faster."

"Already thought of that," the sheriff said. "It's not here. His son, Ryan, flew the senator to Houston for some sort of medical tests. Not expected back for a couple of days."

There'd been rumors for months that in addition to financial problems the old man was suffering from macular degeneration. Maybe the gossip was true. Ethan had no love for the man and wouldn't shed too many tears over his financial woes, but he didn't wish blindness on anyone.

He dug into his pocket for his truck keys. "I'll help you look for the boy, Sheriff. I know the country around here better than anyone. After all, we used to own it."

"I'll help, too," Kayla said.

"There's no need—"

"A boy's life is in danger," she interrupted. "Of course there's a need."

"Can I go, too?" Megan begged. "My voice is better. I can call out for him."

The sheriff smiled. "That's very thoughtful—"

"No," Kayla replied sharply, and saw her daughter pull back. She softened her tone. "I need you and Grandpa to do something here. Phone all the kids in your class and ask them if they've seen Brad or if they know where he might have gone. Find out if anyone knows anything about his aunt Betty, what her last name is, where she lives, or if there are any other people he talked about. Will you do that?"

"Okay," Megan mumbled, pleased to have a role, but disappointed that she wouldn't be going anywhere.

"Grab your cell phone and a hat," Ethan told Kayla. "We'll drive over to my place. You can take the Mule—"

"You're going to ride a mule?" Megan asked in awe.

Ethan snorted. "The Kawasaki Mule." He turned back to her mother. "You can follow the perimeter fence. I'll explain where to check more closely. I'll ride Cinco cross-country on the most likely route Brad would take, assuming he knows directions. It's supposed to hit the century mark today. We'll need to take plenty of water, both for us and for him. There aren't any streams in his likely path, and all the windmills on the old spread are shut off. If he's out there, we need to find him quick, before he gets heatstroke."

Kayla's hands shook as she retrieved the cell phone from her purse and clipped it to her waistband. She grabbed the straw hat she usually wore in the vineyard and put it on.

"Dad, call me if you find out anything."

"I will, and I want you to call me every

twenty minutes to let me know where you are. Don't be reckless, sweetheart. We don't need any more casualties."

She kissed him on the cheek, then bent and gave Megan a big hug. "Thanks for helping with the phone calls, honey."

"Will Brad be all right?" Megan asked, finally realizing how serious the situation was.

"We're going to do everything we can to make sure he is."

She just hoped they'd find him in time.

CHAPTER FIFTEEN

KAYLA FOLLOWED ETHAN OVER to the Broken Spoke, where they found Luella in the kitchen filling water jugs at the sink. "The sheriff was here," she said over her shoulder. "The boy's run away."

"We just saw Wade," Ethan told her. He surveyed the collection of plastic gallon bottles. "What's this?"

"You are going to look for him, aren't you?"

He let out a soft chuckle and lightly draped an arm on her shoulder. "You know me too well. Where's Carter?"

The sound of booted feet on the porch made Kayla turn. The ranch hand placed a pair of saddlebags on the porch rail and came to the screen door.

"Packed the usual stuff," the older man said. "First aid kit, bandages, tools and food. It's hot as blazes out there today. I hope that boy had enough sense to wear a cap and take water with him."

"So do I," Ethan said, "but if he did take anything to drink I'm sure it wasn't enough."

"I figure you'll want to take Cinco. I'll take Pronto." He looked at Kayla with a dubious expression. "You going, too?"

She nodded, but before she had a chance to speak, Ethan said, "She'll take the Mule." He glanced at the plastic jugs Luella was filling from the tap. "How many—"

"Twenty," she said, "but I have more out in the shed if we need them. It'll only take me a minute to—"

"Carter and I will take six apiece on horseback. Kayla can take the other eight in the mule. You'd better get more ready after we leave, though. Just in case."

Luella nodded.

"How do you want to split up?" Carter asked.

"Let's go into the office." Ethan led the way through the dining room to the den off the living room and stepped up to an old map on the wall behind the desk. For the first time, Kayla saw the outline of the Broken Spoke ranch the way it had been and the old K-bar-C that had constituted KC Enterprises. The only spread larger was the Four Aces, which adjoined it on the southwest.

Ethan traced the road along the eastern edge

of the former consortium property line. "This is the road the school bus takes every day. It's the route Brad's most familiar with. There's a good chance he'll try to follow it, but if he went on the road itself, the sheriff would have found him by now."

"Unless he was picked up as a hitchhiker," the ranch hand grumbled.

It was a possibility Kayla didn't like to contemplate. Good people picked up hitchhikers, but so did others.

"If someone he knew gave him a lift, the sheriff would probably know by now, since there's an Amber alert out for him. If it was a stranger..." He let the words trail off. "We'll assume he wasn't thumbing his way. He's a smart kid, so he might be following the road he's familiar with on the inside of the fence."

Ethan ran his hand along a wide swath adjacent to the public road.

"There are several places along the route—" he pointed to specific locations "—where he could hole up and never be seen. Best way to check them out is on horseback."

He turned to Kayla. "I'd like you to take this perimeter road." He drew his finger along the western edge of the old property line. "Check out the culverts and wooden bridges over the streambeds. Here, here and here. They'll probably be dry, since we haven't had any rain in several weeks. Those are also the only places where he'll find decent shade."

He looked at his watch. Almost three o'clock. "By now I imagine he's very thirsty. Unfortunately there's no water along either of those trails."

Kayla bit her lip.

Ethan tapped a spot on the southern edge of the map. "He probably entered the ranchland here. It's less than a quarter mile from the Rayborns' house. From there he could follow the long, roundabout perimeter roads or try to blaze a shortcut directly through the spread. Nasty terrain that way, but he'd have no way of knowing that."

"You figure he'll go for a straight shot?" Carter asked.

"He's a boy on the run, with a mobility problem, and smart enough to opt for the most direct route to his target."

Ethan made a broad sweep of the middle of the spread with his hand. "I'll cover as much of this central corridor as I can and hope the kid decided to stay on trails." He ran a fingernail along the dotted line that represented a dirt road. "I don't know how far he would get with that foot of his. I just hope he didn't venture too far off. Any questions?"

"What do we do if we find him?" Kayla asked.

"If he's all right, call your dad so he can spread the word and bring him in. If he's hurt or unconscious, dial 911. They'll want you to stay on the line until help arrives, but ask them to contact your dad so he can reach us."

She nodded.

"Okay, let's go."

KAYLA CONTINUED ALONG the dusty trail that paralleled the barbed-wire fence separating the Four Aces from the original Broken Spoke. It didn't seem likely Brad would go this way, since it would be totally unfamiliar to him. On the other hand, that might add to its appeal.

The first place Ethan had indicated where Brad could take refuge from the broiling sun was a red rock overhang that faced north and was therefore always in shade. The boy wasn't there, nor was there any indication anyone had been recently. This was still miles from the Rayborns' house, however, so it wasn't likely he'd have gotten this far. Kayla moved on.

Eight minutes later she arrived at the second location, a culvert formed by a dry streambed.

The wood-plank bridge over it furnished good cover. She slowed the Mule and carefully negotiated the steep bank. No sign of Brad.

She was about to continue when her eye caught a glint under a pile of windblown tumbleweeds. She left the engine running and got off the Mule to investigate. Plastic bottles. Even without the weeds covering them they would have been invisible to anyone traveling on the plank bridge overhead and probably wouldn't have been seen by a casual hiker, either.

She'd already glimpsed a familiar label. Roundup. On the edge of the collection was a spray applicator. There was no reason for any of this to be here, of course. No legitimate reason.

ETHAN MOVED as fast as the terrain allowed, setting Cinco at a loose trot when the land was flat and unobstructed, slowing to a near crawl when they reached rocky, uneven ground. Using a horse in the search had several advantages. It allowed him to cover terrain inaccessible by ground vehicle, even for the versatile Mule or a motorcycle. It also gave him better speed than if he were on foot. Not to mention the perspective of height.

So far the young gelding was doing beautifully, apparently enjoying the adventure of being out on the open prairie. Ethan would have to guard against overtaxing him in the heat.

He'd already checked out three possible rest areas. Nothing. He and Kayla had talked on the phone once, apprising each other of their positions. She hadn't found anything, either.

Perhaps he was wrong in assuming Brad was headed for the Broken Spoke, but he didn't think so. The boy came alive when he was at the ranch, working with "his" horse. The kid was smart, though his schoolwork until recently hadn't shown it. Given the traumas he'd been through, it was a wonder he was functional at all. Ethan couldn't imagine anyone, much less a father, abusing a child the way Brad's father had abused him, or a mother standing by and letting it happen. There were bad people in the world. The amazing part was that they could produce good kids like Brad.

He thought about Kayla, about what she'd gone through with her husband. Daryl was another example of someone who wasn't worthy of the precious gift he'd been given. A child. A daughter.

Ahead, Ethan spied a windmill. Several of its blades were twisted, a few missing. The sight filled him with a sense of shame. Failure. No one had been performing maintenance

on the place—their place—since it had gone
bust three years ago. Windmills, while envi-
ronmentally friendly, were low-volume, high-
maintenance items, which was why so many
ranchers had replaced them with more efficient
and dependable electric pumps where power
was readily available.

Approaching it from high ground, Ethan
could see the circular concrete tank was empty.
Weeds had sprouted inside it from windblown
seeds that had found a foothold in the dust
that was filling it in. Over the years their roots
would chip away at the concrete bottom, eventually fracturing it. The walls would split, making the structure useless, and eventually the
site would become a ruin, an artifact of man's
vain attempt to control nature. In the end the
land always won.

Dismissing these maudlin thoughts, Ethan
rode around to the shady side of the tank. He
was sweating and longed to stop for a few minutes' respite from the broiling sun, but delay
could be fatal if he didn't find the boy soon. A
drink from his canteen would have to suffice.

Then he saw it, stretched out along the base
of the tank. A form. The body of a young boy.

KAYLA'S FIRST REACTION was outrage.

She counted the bottles. A dozen. Six of them

empty, another six with unbroken seals. Did that mean the culprit was planning to come back and poison her vineyard again?

The sheriff wanted proof that a crime had been committed. Well, now he'd have his evidence. Clearly this cache was clandestine. There was no other reason for it to be here. The next question was where would this lead. Would it help discover who was out to destroy her?

She couldn't dwell on this mystery now. That would have to wait. Once again she looked around for any indication Brad might be hiding here. He wasn't, and she didn't think he ever had been.

She climbed back onto the Mule. As she chugged out from under the old structure, she made careful note of where she was so she could pass the information to her father on her next call in. No real hurry. This stuff had been here for a while and didn't pose an immediate threat.

Surely there was a code on the labels the sheriff could use to track down the buyer.

ETHAN QUICKLY DISMOUNTED and threw Cinco's reins over a mesquite limb. The horse wasn't likely to run off, but he didn't want to take any chances.

He knelt at Brad's side and pressed his fingers to his neck. The boy was breathing, and a prayer of thanksgiving rose to Ethan's lips. He felt for a pulse. It seemed slow.

Ethan ran to Cinco, grabbed one of the water jugs and raced back. The boy's complexion was red, his skin dry, lips parched. Ethan saw he'd removed his prosthetic foot. It lay on the ground beside him. He pulled up the jeans leg and looked at the stump. Raw and bloody.

He poured a good deal of the water over the boy's shirt and face, then gently lifted his head and tried to give him some to drink. It just flowed down his cheeks.

Ethan grabbed the cell phone from his belt and hit the fast dial for Kayla's phone. She answered on the second ring.

"I found him," he said hurriedly. "At the tank in Turkey Draw. I'm calling 911 now, so this line will be tied up. Pass the word to your dad and the sheriff."

"Is he all right?"

"He's alive but unconscious. I'll call you back as soon as I can." He cut the connection and pressed 911.

"I've found Brad Estes," he told the dispatcher and gave what information he could.

"Can we get a vehicle in there?"

"Not easily. Part of the dirt road that comes here from my place has been washed out, probably in that big storm we had last fall. There isn't any other road access to this spot. Going around it won't be easy. Lots of debris blocking the way and the cactus is hip-high. Best bet is coming in by chopper."

"We'll check with the National Guard, see if there's one available."

"Hurry. His pulse is weak, his breathing shallow. He needs help sooner rather than later."

"Any other injuries?"

Ethan put down the cell phone while he performed a cursory examination. "No broken bones or other wounds I can see. He's an amputee, though, missing one foot. He's removed the prosthesis. The stump's a mess, but he's not bleeding anywhere else as far as I can tell."

He heard voices in the background, then the person at the other end came back on the line. "Chopper's on the way. How will the pilot know where to find you?"

"We've always called this place Turkey Draw, but I don't think it's marked on any topographical map." Ethan gave directions as clearly as he could, using his ranch house as one reference point and Clint Gallagher's hilltop hacienda as another.

"I'm at a windmill. We're on the north side of the tank, in the shade. I have a horse with me." Then he came up with an idea. "There's some dry brush in the tank. I'll see if I can set it ablaze. Your pilot won't have any trouble seeing the smoke."

"Good. That'll make it easier."

Which reminded Ethan he'd better tie Cinco more securely, in case the smoke and the chopper spooked him.

"Is there adequate space to land?"

Ethan stood and surveyed the area. "On the east side. Terrain is fairly flat. A few small mesquite and a few cedars, but I think there's enough room."

"Okay, they're airborne now. Estimated time of arrival…ten minutes. Leave this line open."

Ethan wished he had a hands-free model. He hooked the cell phone on his belt and poured more water on the nine-year-old, hoping to bring down his body temperature. Again, he tried to coax some down his throat. It produced a cough, which he took as a positive sign, but didn't want to take the chance of drowning the kid.

He got up and made his way to Cinco, reassured the gelding with words and gentle pats, then fastened his reins securely to a stronger limb of the mesquite. From a saddlebag he removed matches from the survival kit Carter had packed, and walked over to the rickety wooden ladder on the side of the tank.

Dead grass and tumbleweeds dotted the uneven bottom. He wondered what else might be lurking there. Scorpions, snakes, the possibilities were too numerous to catalogue. He piled the brush together and lit a match. It didn't catch, but the second one did. He tore out some bindweed and tossed it into the hot blaze, as well.

He was just climbing over the top of the wall when he heard the unmistakable drone of a helicopter. Looking up, he saw it headed directly for the plume of grayish-white smoke rising lethargically into the clear blue sky.

He hurried back to the boy. Brad's breathing was still shallow and a finger to his carotid artery indicated his heartbeat was also still slow. Had the boy merely passed out from exhaustion or had he suffered a heatstroke?

The chopper landed right where Ethan had suggested. The noise and dust made Cinco dance, but he turned his back to the commotion and didn't try very hard to escape. Ethan really didn't want to have to go chase him later.

Paramedics appeared around the side of the circular tank while Ethan was still huddled over the boy, shielding him from the dust and debris whirling around them. One medic carried an aluminum suitcase, which he set down next to the boy. The other quickly expanded a stretcher. Ethan backed off to give them access.

The first man took vital signs.

"Temperature one-oh-one. Pulse thirty-four. Thready. Respiration shallow and eighteen." He read the self-inflating cuff he'd put on Brad's small upper arm. "BP ninety-eight over thirty-eight." He ran his hands over the patient's body. "No signs of physical trauma. Start IV. Run it open, then let's move."

The second man had already positioned the stretcher closer. He inserted the intravenous needle in the boy's left arm and taped it in place. Temporarily placing the bag of Ringer's lactate on the patient's chest, they lifted the unconscious child onto the pallet.

"You coming with us?" he asked Ethan.

"Yes." He realized he was still connected to 911. "Can I use a cell phone in the chopper? My horse—"

"Make your call now. I'll give you thirty seconds."

Ethan requested the dispatcher contact his ranch—he gave the number—and ask Carter Dunlap to come by and get the horse. He hated leaving Cinco alone but knew the gelding would be safe for the hour it might take the ranch hand to reach him.

He hoped the sheriff would be in touch with Kayla and let her know what was happening.

AS SOON AS SHE GOT THE CALL from Ethan, Kayla turned the Mule around and headed back to the ranch house. She gave the utility vehicle full throttle, her mind filled with unanswered questions. How seriously injured was the boy? Had he fallen, broken a bone or simply passed out from heat exhaustion?

Was he so badly dehydrated he'd suffered a heatstroke? Would they be able to save his life?

She calculated he'd been missing at least twelve hours. The sun had been up perhaps nine. Not an exceptionally long time to go without food or water. Under ordinary circumstances he'd just be hungry and very thirsty, but today hadn't been ordinary. The temperature had hit a hundred degrees, the hottest Kayla had ever endured. A stifling, dry, baking heat that dried her mouth and sinuses to the point of pain. She was thankful Megan was home in the air-conditioned house with her grandfather.

She wondered how Ethan was faring. He cared very deeply for Brad, just as he did for Heather and Megan. He had so much love to give…

The mule hit a bump, bucked and went airborne, making Kayla's heart leap at the same time. She instinctively took her foot off the gas pedal and clutched the wheel with a premonition of impending doom. The vehicle nose-dived onto the gravelly surface and bounced into place, still rolling forward.

Kayla's pulse was pounding, her nerves near the shattering point. She was shaking and wanted to stop but didn't dare. Vowing to pay better attention, she made the turn toward the ranch house.

Luella came out on the porch as Kayla approached. Kayla shut off the engine and jumped out at a run. "Any more word?"

"The dispatcher called, said the helicopter was there—"

"What helicopter? Gallagher's?"

"Rescue."

"Where's Ethan?"

"Gone with the boy to San Antonio. Carter's bringing in Ethan's horse."

"Is Brad all right?"

Luella shrugged. "No one knows."

That wasn't what Kayla wanted to hear. Still, it could have been worse. "What hospital?"

"The medical center, I think."

"I'll find out. I'm going home to get my car, but I also need to speak to the sheriff. Do you know where he is?"

"I haven't heard."

"I'll call him from home. I need to make sure Megan is all right, first."

The five-minute drive to the vineyard took four. Kayla skidded the Toyota to a halt in a cloud of white dust and ran into the house.

"Is Brad going to be all right?" Megan asked the minute Kayla stepped inside.

"I hope so, honey. Ethan found him quickly, so that's good, and they're taking him to San Antonio, to the hospital where you were."

"Will Dr. Hernandez be there? She's nice."

"I don't know. It's a big hospital." She turned to her dad. "I found a stash of herbicide that I think was used to poison the vineyard."

His eyes went wide. "Where?"

"Hidden in a culvert about two miles from here."

"Why on Ethan's old ranch?"

"Dad, you're not suggesting he might have had something to do with what happened, are you?"

He looked pained. "Of course not. What I'm asking is who would think to use his old ranch to hide this stuff?"

"Trying to frame him? I hadn't thought of that," she admitted. "I figured it was just a convenient out-of-the-way spot."

"And maybe it was, but until we find out who did it, we won't know."

"Dad, Ethan flew on the rescue chopper with Brad to the medical center in San Antonio. I'm going to join him there."

CHAPTER SIXTEEN

IN THE TIME IT TOOK ETHAN to make his telephone call, the paramedics had a line in Brad's arm and were giving him much-needed fluids. The boy had moaned and squirmed halfheartedly, which relieved Ethan. The only thing better would have been if he'd awakened.

He scrambled aboard the helicopter, closed the door and they were airborne. The medics had headphones in their helmets and were talking to each other, but the cabin was too noisy for Ethan to hear what they were saying. He watched with both admiration and apprehension as they monitored their young patient.

Faster than he'd expected, they landed on a helipad. A medical team met them and quickly moved Brad inside. One of them asked Ethan, "What can you tell us about him?"

"Nine years old, ran away from his foster home sometime during the night. When I found him he was unconscious."

"What about that foot? How did he lose it?"

"Amputated a few years ago as a result of parental abuse." The guy didn't blink at the information. "He'd already taken the prosthesis off when I found him. Judging from the looks of the stump it must hurt like mad."

"So it was trauma, not disease. Are you aware of any allergies, other medical conditions we should know about?"

"He's not diabetic, I know that, but the person who can probably give you the history you need is Leona Rayborn, his foster mother in Homestead."

"We'll contact her."

That would take time. "If it'll help, I can call her."

"Good. We need the information ASAP."

Ethan started to use his cell phone.

"Not in here. Use the phone at the desk or go outside."

"Gotcha. I just need to get the number from a friend."

"No one remembers telephone numbers anymore," the guy muttered as he walked away.

The nurse at the emergency room desk gave him an outside line and he punched in Kayla's cell number. She answered on the second ring. Incredibly the sound of her voice calmed him.

"We're at the hospital," he said. "Brad's still

unconscious, but they're pumping him full of fluids. I need to find out his medical history from Leona. Do you have her number, or should I contact the sheriff and have him track her down?"

"I've got it," she said. "Let me check my contacts list."

Remembering the medic's comment, Ethan almost smiled. A few seconds later she rattled off a number. He jotted it down on a pad by the phone.

"Is he going to be all right?" she asked.

"I hope so. Where are you?"

"In my car on my way. I should be there in about fifteen minutes."

"Drive safely. I'll be waiting." He wanted to add *I love you*. But he didn't. Maybe it was because of where he was and the people around him. Maybe because he'd never said those words to a woman other than his mother and sister. Maybe because he wanted to say them to Kayla in person rather than over the phone....

He disconnected and dialed Leona. She answered on the fourth ring. A baby was crying in the background. He identified himself and told her where he was and why.

"You found him, then." She exhaled audibly. "How is he? Going to be okay?"

"He's unconscious. The doctors are working on him now. They need to know his medical history."

"Other than the foot, he isn't—"

"I'm going to put the nurse on and let her ask you the questions, rather than relay them."

"Okay. And, Mr. Ritter, thank you." The sincerity in her voice made him rethink his earlier harsh judgment of her.

He turned the phone over to the woman standing beside him and gave her Leona's name. Then he went looking for the team working on Brad. To his relief Dr. Hernandez appeared.

"You're getting to be a regular here." They shook hands.

"How is he?"

"It'll be a while before we know for sure. Any idea how long he was unconscious?"

"No, but I can tell you he was missing not much more than fifteen hours, and based on where I found him, I'd say he spent most of that walking."

"The less time he was unconscious the better. From what we can tell so far, he seems to be suffering mostly from dehydration. What can you tell me about his foot?"

He recounted the story of his father nailing it

to the floor to discipline him, resulting in gangrene and amputation.

"How long ago was that?"

"About three years, I think."

"He's going to need a new prosthesis once the stump heals. The one he has is too small. Didn't anyone notice he was limping?"

Ethan looked away, feeling guilty. "I asked him once if it hurt him. He said it was fine. He didn't limp all the time. I figured it would be normal for him to limp if he'd had it on a long time or was very active."

"At his age, he outgrows them as fast as a pair of shoes, but with a well-fitted prosthesis, he shouldn't even notice that he has one. In fact, he should be able to play most sports without discomfort."

"He hasn't had a very happy childhood," Ethan said. "He probably accepted it hurting as natural."

She shook her head, but said nothing.

The next person through the door was the sheriff striding toward them. Ethan introduced Wade to the doctor, who then received a page, excused herself and left. Ethan gave Wade a rundown of events.

"You seem to have a knack for saving children," Wade commented.

"I'd like it a lot better if they didn't need saving."

"I just got through talking to Leona Rayborn. You beat me to her."

"Is she coming?"

"I offered her a lift, but she has five other kids to take care of."

"About his dad—" Ethan began.

"Already talked to the district attorney. He's going to get a restraining order to keep him away from the boy. If Carn Estes calls Brad or comes within spitting distance, he goes back to prison."

Ethan exhaled. "Thanks."

Kayla barged through the door. She looked worried and angry. As far as Ethan was concerned, even hot and disheveled, she was absolutely beautiful. He wanted to lock her in his arms and crush her with a kiss, but contented himself with taking her hand and giving her an affectionate peck on the cheek.

The same questions and answers followed.

"I found something you'll be interested in," Kayla told the sheriff. "While I was out searching for Brad, I discovered a cache of herbicide, Roundup to be exact, in a culvert on the old Broken Spoke spread. An applicator, too. Half of the bottles are empty, the other half, full."

She smiled at Ethan. "Seems like you and Dad staying up all night to guard the new shipment was a good idea."

Ethan nodded. "Sure does."

Wade asked for specific directions to the site.

Ethan immediately recognized the location she described. "I should have thought of that spot," he said. "Secluded, but easy access to your vineyard. Not far from the Four Aces, either. Did you see any breaks in the fence?"

She shook her head. "I also didn't touch anything," she told the sheriff. "Thought you might be able to check the stuff for fingerprints."

"I'll get right on it." With that he tipped his hat, reached for the cell phone on his belt and disappeared out the door.

Ethan turned to Kayla. They were alone in the same small waiting area they'd shared the night before, with no guarantee the privacy would last.

"I'm glad you came," he said softly, cupping his hands around the back of her neck and touching his forehead to hers.

"I couldn't stay away," she muttered.

He spread his arms and she slipped into them. Holding her close felt so right. The touch, the warmth she brought to him was a fulfillment he never wanted to give up.

"I can't believe all this is happening," she murmured.

"Neither can I, but I know it's right."

She shifted and gazed up in shock.

"I was talking about us," he explained. "About you and me. Have I gotten it all wrong?"

"Mommy, Mommy—"

Kayla spun around to the open doorway in time to catch her daughter in her arms.

"Sweetheart—" Kayla scooped her up "—what are you doing here?"

"We came to see if Brad is okay. Did he get sunburned?"

Kayla laughed. "We haven't gotten to visit with him yet, so I don't know, but he probably did."

"I bet he didn't put on sunscreen like I always do. Boys can be so dumb—"

"He's not dumb," Heather declared from the doorway, where she was standing beside Kayla's father. "It's not his fault."

Megan scowled with the knowing look in her eyes of a woman twenty years older.

"Megan insisted we come to see Brad, to make sure he's okay," Boyd said, as if he hadn't had any choice, "and I figured Heather would be worried about him, too, so I called Leona."

"Heather's going to spend the night with us," Megan added.

Kayla was touched by her father's thoughtfulness.

"Can we see him now?" Megan asked.

"Let me find out," Kayla said.

With perfect timing, Lou Hernandez appeared in the doorway behind Boyd. "I thought you'd like to know Brad is awake."

"How is he?" Kayla asked for all of them. "Is he going to be all right?"

"We still need to monitor him for a bit, but he appears to be fine. The kid's tough," she said with a smile of approval.

Ethan reached for Kayla's hand. "Are we allowed in to see him?"

"No reason why not. A few familiar faces is just what he needs about now."

Brad's eyes brightened when he saw his friends, but he looked sheepish when he saw the adults behind them.

"Thank you for finding me," he said to Ethan. "I didn't mean to—"

"You're okay." Ethan rested his hand on Brad's shoulder. "That's all that matters."

Kayla leaned over and gave him a kiss on the cheek and told him how glad she was that he was all right.

"Luella insisted I tell you she's making your favorite chocolate chip cookies," Boyd said with a grin. "So you better get well quick, before somebody else eats them."

"My dad—"

"Don't worry about him," Ethan told the boy. "He won't be bothering you anymore. I promise."

Brad fought back tears, probably not wanting to admit just how afraid of him he was.

While the children visited, Ethan and Kayla slipped out of the room with the doctor.

"When will you be discharging him?" Kayla asked.

"We need to keep him under observation overnight," Lou replied. "Unless something unforeseen develops, though, we should be able to release him in the morning." Another page sent her running.

Kayla spoke up. "Since Leona's letting Heather spend tonight with us, why don't I call her and ask if she'll extend it for a few days. If she says yes—and I bet she will, considering all the packing she has to do—I'll ask her if Dad and I can take Brad home with us tomorrow. He'll just be an extra burden for her. It'll also make it harder for Brad's father to get to him."

Ethan grinned. "Smart lady. That's even better than my plan."

"Which was?"

"To ask Dr. Hernandez to keep him here for a few more days."

"Why would she do that? There's no medical justification—"

He held up their joined hands. "To give us enough time to get married and apply for permanent custody of him."

"Married?"

"You asked me to marry you, and now I'm giving you my final answer. It's yes. If you still want me, that is."

"Of course I do—" she blurted out, then broke off when she realized what she was saying. "But—"

"There is one thing, though," he said, his lips close to her mouth. "I don't want a marriage of convenience, Kayla. I want to be with you for the rest of my life."

"I…I don't know what to say."

"Say yes. Say you'll marry me." He gazed into her eyes. "I've tried to fight my feelings, Kayla, but it's no use. I'm in love with you."

Her face split into a conspiratorial grin. "While we're at the courthouse getting a marriage license, we better file for a restraining order, too."

"A restraining order?" To keep him away from her? Surely...

She stared at him, grinning mischievously, then laughed, clearly enjoying his discomfort.

"Against Child Protective Services," she explained, "forbidding them from taking Brad or Heather out of the county or my...our house until the matter of their adoption is finalized."

Ethan pulled her into his arms. "You're brilliant." He kissed her. A real kiss, one that would have led to many more if they hadn't been standing in the middle of the hallway of a public hospital.

"IS HE REALLY ALL RIGHT?" Leona asked over the phone.

Kayla thought she heard the huskiness that goes with tears in the question. "The others are with him now. He's fine. A bit sunburned, and his stump is a mess, but the doc assures us it'll heal and he'll be fine as soon as he can be fitted with a new foot."

"I'm glad you're there for him. I should be," Leona admitted, "but Randy's still in Chicago checking out housing, so I'm all by myself. And

piling all the kids into the car to take them into
San Antonio—"

"You've got your hands full. Thanks for letting Heather stay overnight with us. Megan is
ecstatic. Would you mind if she stayed a couple of days?"

"I don't see why not. It'll actually be easier
with her away."

"Then I'd like to ask you one other favor, if
I may."

"Anything."

"They'll be releasing Brad tomorrow morning. Would it be all right if we took him home
with us, too? Dad and I can keep both of them a
few days, at least until your husband gets back.
I don't know if you were counting on him to
help with your packing, but he wouldn't be able
to do much with just one foot, and at least he
won't be in your way."

There was a brief pause, then a little laugh.
"You're going to try to keep them, aren't you?"

Kayla hesitated, not sure she should admit it.

Leona laughed again. "Good. They deserve
better." There was a note of regret in the statement, making Kayla wonder how much it was
costing the childless woman. After another moment of silence, she said, "Keep them both with
you as long as you want."

"Thank you," Kayla said, her eyes misting over.

"Might be a good way for you to decide if you really want to take on the job full-time," Leona added. "Randy and I won't be leaving for another two weeks at least, maybe longer, if he can't find us a decent place. After that… Well, you seem more than capable of fighting your own battles. Oh, be sure to stop by and I'll give you some of their clothes."

"Thank you, Leona," Kayla said sincerely.

"No need to thank me. Just the opposite. You're helping me, remember?"

The announcement that Brad and Heather would be staying at Megan's house for a while had the kids jumping with joy. The following morning Brad was released on crutches, after being given an appointment to be fitted for a new prosthesis as soon as his stump healed. He would also start a new round of physical therapy to make sure he could use it properly.

They drove home in Ethan's pickup, he and Kayla up front, the three children in the backseat. They sang at the top of their lungs all the way to Homestead.

Boyd was waiting for them when they arrived. He and Carter had spent the morning moving extra beds from Ethan's place to Kayla's. She'd been using the tiny fourth bedroom as her office. For the time being at least, her computer desk and file cabinets had to be crammed into her bedroom. Megan and Heather would share Megan's bedroom, and Brad would have his own room, a luxury he'd never had before.

The children were chattering away at the kitchen table, and Boyd was grilling cheese sandwiches, when Ethan invited Kayla into the backyard.

The sun was shining. A soft, warm breeze wafted across the covered patio. He took her in his arms and gazed down into her blue eyes.

"I love you, Kayla."

She snuggled against him. "I love you, too."

"I don't deserve you," he confessed. "I'll always be grateful—"

"Shh—" She covered his lips with a fingertip. "I don't want gratitude," she whispered. "Just give me your love. That's enough."

He kissed her then. *I'll spend the rest of my life trying to be worthy of you,* he vowed.

EPILOGUE

Three months later

KAYLA WAS WALKING alongside a little girl with spina bifida on a pony Ethan had bought a few weeks earlier when she saw the sheriff's car pull up. Wade got out, strolled in his loose-limbed way over to the fence and leaned his elbows on the top rail. He'd been best man at the wedding performed by Noah six weeks earlier.

She smiled at the memory of the sun streaming through the stained glass windows and the pipe organ making the marble floor vibrate under her feet as she'd marched down the aisle on her father's arm. The room filled with the wonderful scent of beeswax candles. The gathering had been small, but that lent to the intimacy of the ceremony that united her with Ethan Ritter for the rest of their lives.

She motioned to one of the many volunteers Noah had recruited to take her place and wandered over to the fence.

Wade tilted his head to the three handicapped children riding in a large circle in the middle of the area. Each had a volunteer on both sides guiding and encouraging them.

"They look happy," he said. "You're doing a great job with them."

"It's one of the most satisfying things I've ever done. Couldn't do it without all the volunteers Noah has recruited, though."

They stood watching in silence for several minutes. Eventually Ethan broke away from the deaf boy he was coaching and joined them.

"What brings you out here?" he asked.

"Just thought you might like a progress report."

"About Tolly?" Kayla asked.

Wade nodded.

The fingerprints on the herbicide Kayla had found turned out to be those of Tolliver Craddock, the maintenance man at Megan's school. He'd been a suspect in a robbery a few years back, so his fingerprints were on file. The sheriff had arrested him on charges of felonious mischief and grand theft and thrown him into jail.

The evidence against the forty-year-old handyman had been overwhelming. Wade had been able to trace the sale of the herbicide to a nursery in San Antonio. The store owner had identified Craddock in a lineup as the person who had purchased it. Craddock had denied it, of course, but his fingerprints were the only ones found on the plastic jugs. The case against him was solid, yet it still lacked closure.

Why had he done it? And how had a janitor gotten the cash to buy over a thousand dollars' worth of expensive herbicide? Clearly the guy hadn't done this on his own. He had no motive to target Kayla or her vineyard. But Craddock had steadfastly refused to say who'd hired him.

"He has a new lawyer," the sheriff said.

He'd been represented by a public defender at the arraignment. "Who?" Ethan asked.

"A high-priced mouthpiece from Austin by the name of Raoul Dermody. He put up a bond for Craddock this morning. We had to release him a couple of hours ago."

Ethan made a growling sound.

"Who's Raoul Dermody?" Kayla asked a moment later. "Never heard of him."

"You probably never heard of Johnnie Cochran before the O.J. case, either."

Ethan shrugged. "And your point is?"

"Craddock's a loser who couldn't afford Dermody in the first place. In the second, Dermody doesn't normally take on lowlifes like him as clients. Yet now, all of a sudden, Craddock has the resources to post a bond for a fifty-thousand-dollar bail. It all confirms my suspicion that someone else was behind the poisoning."

"So what do you reckon will happen now?"

"Craddock's crime isn't all that serious. No one was hurt. No one threatened. No weapon or illegal substances were involved. My guess is that Dermody will either get him off with a suspended sentence or if he is sent to prison it'll be for a minimum time, and there'll be a tidy sum waiting for him in a checking account somewhere when he's released. Unless the D.A. is willing to play hardball."

"How do you mean?" Ethan asked.

The lawman hesitated for a moment. "When we checked Craddock's workshop in the basement of the school, we found something curious, a caged cat."

"To catch mice?" Kayla paused. "But why keep it in a cage?"

"Maybe he just kept it caged during the day, when kids are around," Ethan speculated, "and let it out at night."

Wade shook his head. "There's a school policy against having any animals in the school, and there's every indication he never released it. We checked his vacuum cleaner. It was full of cat hair."

"Then why—" Kayla frowned. "Wait. You're not suggesting... Megan..."

The sheriff nodded. "We examined her desk in the classroom. The back corners of it, out of sight, were filled with cat hair and dander."

Kayla clasped Ethan's hand. "That explains why she got so sick when I kept her home. She'd just opened the workbook she'd brought from school."

Ethan's face went rigid. "So her attack wasn't from pecan tassels," he said through clenched teeth.

Wade turned to Kayla. "You recently had her tested. Did pecan tassels show up?"

"Yes, but not nearly as strongly as we'd expected. But this…this explains a lot."

"Help me out here," Ethan said, his brow furrowed.

Kayla looked up at him. "Megan is highly allergic to cats, and she's moderately allergic to pecan tassels. The combination, however, has the potential to be lethal. Almost was."

Ethan muttered a vicious word and took a deep breath. "He nearly killed her."

"And that's where the D.A. comes in," Wade told him. "He's considering bringing a charge of attempted murder against Craddock as a way of putting pressure on him to reveal the person he's working for."

"Only considering? Why isn't he doing it?" Ethan nearly shouted.

"Because it'll be a tough charge to make stick, especially with a mouthpiece like Raoul Dermody representing him. Proving Craddock knew Megan was allergic to cats is easy, the evidence stands for itself, but proving he knew she was allergic to pecan tassels and that the combination was likely to be deadly is a whole 'nother matter."

After a moment's pause, Ethan grudgingly nodded. "So what's the plan?"

"Wait. Dermody has asked for a trial delay, probably hoping the state will lose interest and drop the charges. In the meantime, there's no reason we can't let this information slip out, make Craddock sweat a little."

"Or skip town."

"There's that possibility, of course. On the other hand, Craddock isn't a genius. I don't think it'll be very hard finding him if he does decide to bolt, and come to think of it, what have we lost if he does disappear for a while? He's not the real target of our investigation or the real culprit, just a handy patsy."

Letting anyone get away wasn't appealing, but Wade had a valid point. "Any ideas who might be paying the bill?" Ethan asked.

Again the sheriff shook his head. "The man with the most clout around here is still the senator."

"There are rumors he's going blind," Ethan said. "Any truth to them?"

"Macular degeneration is what I'm hearing. I doubt he'll be running for office again, which may be making him all the more desperate to get this land. A permanent legacy he can pass on to his kids."

"My dad felt that way once," Ethan muttered.

Kayla reached over and covered his hand with hers.

"Anything more on the adoptions?" Wade asked her.

"Both Brad's parents have relinquished their parental rights. As a matter of fact his father is back in prison for drug violations and will probably remain there for a long time. His mother decided to leave the state, so it looks like clear sailing for both Heather and Brad."

Wade nodded. "I'm glad for them and for you. If you need character witnesses, just say the word. There's a town full of folks who're very proud of both of you."

Kayla smiled. "Thanks. That's nice to know."

Wade left and the last of the special-needs children went home. Megan, Heather and Brad were helping Carter bring horses in from the pasture for the night.

"Where's your dad?" Ethan asked.

"He took Luella over to the old house to show her his bachelor pad."

Ethan smiled. "I think he really likes her cookies."

Kayla laughed. "Are you saying the way to a man's heart is still through his stomach?"

"It was your macaroni and cheese that did it for me."

"And all this time I thought it was my thermos of coffee."

His grin widened. "Yeah, that, too."

The world was at peace, at least for the time being.

Kayla and Ethan went to the kitchen for bottled water from the refrigerator, but before they got that far, he pulled her into his arms.

"Have I told you recently that I love you?"

"I don't know," she said, feigning deep thought. "Seems to me it's been several hours."

"Much too long." He kissed her lips lightly. "I love you, Kayla Ritter."

"I love you, too, Ethan Ritter."

He tightened his hold and kissed her more deeply.

"Umm," she muttered, when they finally broke apart. "Shouldn't you be checking on the horses?"

"They can wait," he whispered in her ear and pulled her closer.

* * * * *

LARGER-PRINT BOOKS!
GET 2 FREE LARGER-PRINT NOVELS PLUS
2 FREE GIFTS!

HARLEQUIN®

Romance

From the Heart, For the Heart

YES! Please send me 2 FREE LARGER-PRINT Harlequin® Romance novels and my 2 FREE gifts (gifts are worth about $10). After receiving them, if I don't wish to receive any more books, I can return the shipping statement marked "cancel." If I don't cancel, I will receive 4 brand-new novels every month and be billed just $4.84 per book in the U.S. or $5.24 per book in Canada. That's a savings of at least 19% off the cover price! It's quite a bargain! Shipping and handling is just 50¢ per book in the U.S. and 75¢ per book in Canada.* I understand that accepting the 2 free books and gifts places me under no obligation to buy anything. I can always return a shipment and cancel at any time. Even if I never buy another book, the two free books and gifts are mine to keep forever.

119/319 HDN F43Y

Name	(PLEASE PRINT)	
Address		Apt. #
City	State/Prov.	Zip/Postal Code

Signature (if under 18, a parent or guardian must sign)

Mail to the **Harlequin® Reader Service:**
IN U.S.A.: P.O. Box 1867, Buffalo, NY 14240-1867
IN CANADA: P.O. Box 609, Fort Erie, Ontario L2A 5X3

Want to try two free books from another line?
Call 1-800-873-8635 or visit www.ReaderService.com.

* Terms and prices subject to change without notice. Prices do not include applicable taxes. Sales tax applicable in N.Y. Canadian residents will be charged applicable taxes. Offer not valid in Quebec. This offer is limited to one order per household. Not valid for current subscribers to Harlequin Romance Larger-Print books. All orders subject to credit approval. Credit or debit balances in a customer's account(s) may be offset by any other outstanding balance owed by or to the customer. Please allow 4 to 6 weeks for delivery. Offer available while quantities last.

Your Privacy—The Harlequin® Reader Service is committed to protecting your privacy. Our Privacy Policy is available online at www.ReaderService.com or upon request from the Harlequin Reader Service.

We make a portion of our mailing list available to reputable third parties that offer products we believe may interest you. If you prefer that we not exchange your name with third parties, or if you wish to clarify or modify your communication preferences, please visit us at www.ReaderService.com/consumerschoice or write to us at Harlequin Reader Service Preference Service, P.O. Box 9062, Buffalo, NY 14269. Include your complete name and address.

HRLP13R

LARGER-PRINT BOOKS!

GET 2 FREE LARGER-PRINT NOVELS PLUS 2 FREE MYSTERY GIFTS

Love Inspired

Larger-print novels are now available...

Reader Service.com

Manage your account online!

- Review your order history
- Manage your payments
- Update your address

> ### We've designed
> ### the Harlequin® Reader Service
> ### website just for you.

Enjoy all the features!

- Reader excerpts from any series
- Respond to mailings and special monthly offers
- Discover new series available to you
- Browse the Bonus Bucks catalog
- Share your feedback

Visit us at:

ReaderService.com